SHAG POINT

AND OTHER STORIES

ROSS DOUGHTY

ILLUSTRATED BY

SARA RANSLEY

Published by Invictus Press

Email: roaldo.nz@gmail.com

A catalogue record for this book is available from the National Library of New Zealand.

ISBN 978-0-473-62412-5 (paperback)

ISBN 978-0-473-62413-2 (EPUB)

Cover illustration by Sara Ransley. Email: sara.ransley@gmail.com

CONTENTS

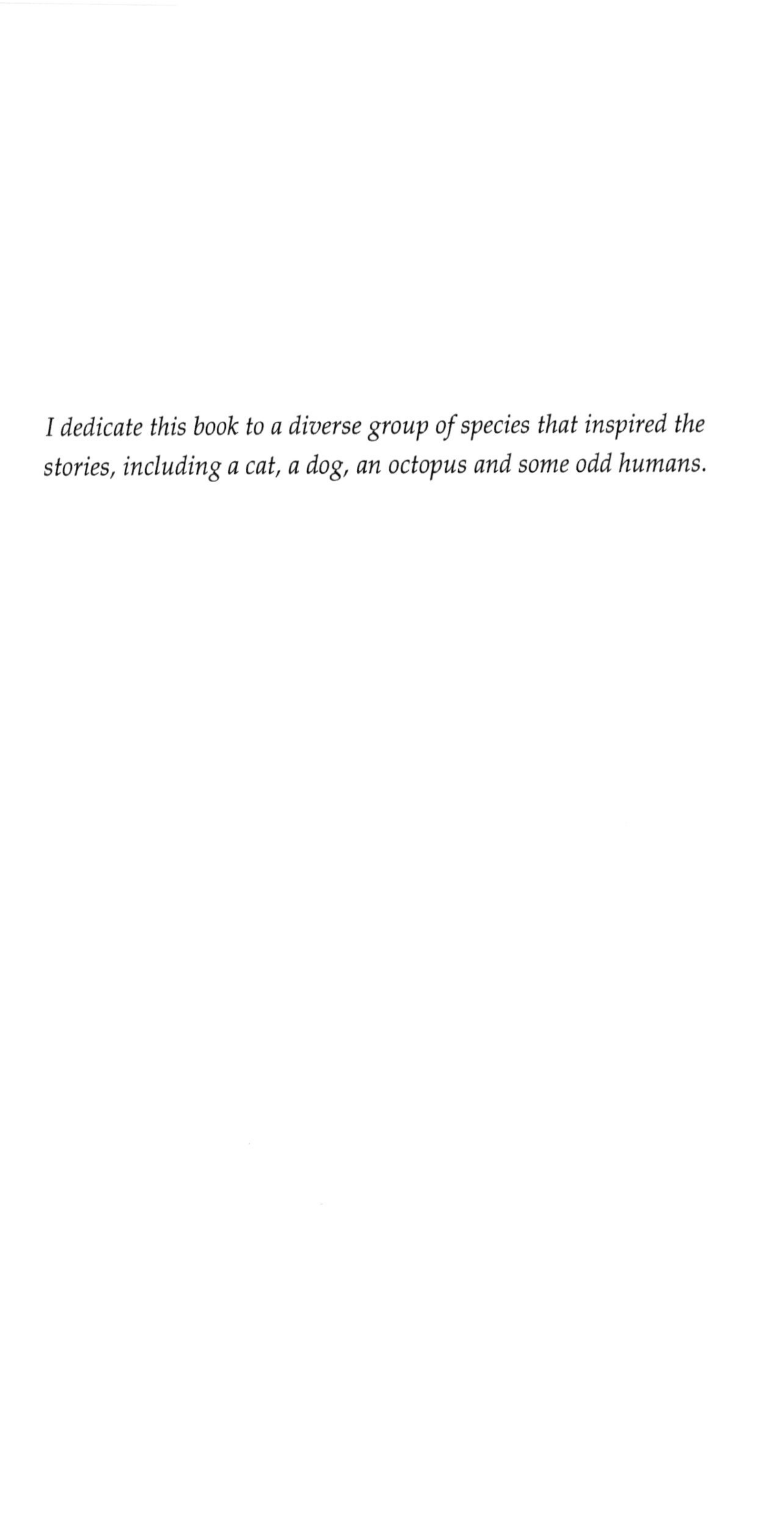

I dedicate this book to a diverse group of species that inspired the stories, including a cat, a dog, an octopus and some odd humans.

MORAL JUDGMENT

THE MOUNT UNDERWATER Club has an annual competition for videos and photography. The contest has different sections: one year, my mate Greg won the Topside Section with a picture of a black shag emerging from Crater

Bay with a piper wriggling in its beak. Earlier, he had won the Club Section with a photo of members having a barbecue on Motiti Island. But he had never won the most prestigious prize, the Underwater Section.

His underwater camera was best for broad 'macro' shots and not capable of 'micro' photos like close-ups of small things like anemones, tiny fish, and other small organisms, and it was those close-up photos that seemed to do best in competitions. He purchased a Go-Pro camera-video recorder, and he could select from the menu of different shots and quickly brought his skills up to speed early in the season, well before the AGM at which the competition was judged.

That did not mean he had given up diving for crayfish or spearing fish; his photography was just another activity he had added to his hunting and gathering. One Saturday, we decided to see if the crayfish had returned to the channel in the harbour entrance after the dredging there some years earlier. We tied the bow rope to the buoy and dived down the 30 metres to the ledges there. Although the structure had changed from how we remembered it, we got our limit of legal-sized crayfish and started ascending slowly to the surface. We stopped to decompress on the anchored line of the buoy in the centre of the channel, and Greg began waving his arms at me.

When I turned, I saw the unforgettable sight of a pod of orcas entering the harbour. They were just a few metres from us. As the surging mass of several of these behemoths passed by us, their enormous eyes, as big as tennis balls, rolled backwards in their sockets as they observed the strange sight of multi-coloured humans bubbling air upwards and waving their limbs. Immediately I thought that Greg would be cursing at not having his brand new camera to catch this once in a lifetime shot that could've won the club's underwater photo of the year for him. Perhaps he would even have entered some of the international competitions with great prizes like overseas trips.

As we surfaced, he surprised me because he wasn't angry at all but enthusiastic, 'Don't you see? They were swimming into the harbour, and they've got to swim out again. That's when we will get photos of them.'

'What do you mean *we*?' I asked. 'I have seen them once; that'll do me!'

He ignored my objections, 'If I remember correctly, they come into the harbour one day, feed on a few stingrays, and go on their merry way the next day. But I'm going to check with a few other divers about that tonight.'

It was as if he had not registered my unwillingness because he took our bottles back to get refilled by our mate at the local dive shop and arranged to pick me up again on Sunday morning. My wife couldn't understand why we wanted to dive back on the same spot the next day. I had told her about seeing the orcas, but not about Greg's plan, so I just said, 'Greg wants to try out his new camera in the entrance.' And that was true enough.

Greg had rung around that night and was still just as excited in the morning, 'Everyone says they swim out on the outgoing tide the day after they arrive. So our timing is perfect. What we'll do is wait in the rubber duck until we see them coming and then go over the side. Right?'

'Right!' I said, but I was a bit nervous. In the channel, we always dived at the turn of the tide when there was no current. The worst time for us to dive was on the outgoing tide. But we were both strong swimmers, super fit, and could always paddle shoreward if the rip was too strong to get back to the boat.

'And I brought both cameras,' he said. 'If something goes

wrong with the new one, you can pass me the old one. That way, I get two chances. If we get separated, shoot some photos yourself. Okay? We should go down the line and hope the pod takes the same path out as when it came in. That way, we won't drift off in the tide.'

That reassured me a little about our actions. He repeatedly checked both cameras while we sat bobbing in the centre of the entrance channel. He turned the switches on and off incessantly and kept sighting through their viewfinders. His nervousness was palpable. I stood at the controls looking towards the container cranes in a forlorn hope of seeing the orcas surfacing and diving like giant dolphins.

When they appeared about 150 metres from us doing exactly that, I was astounded, but Greg wasn't surprised. It was just as he had predicted.

'Right, this is it!' he said and, picking up the new camera, jumped overboard. I picked up the older camera and followed. We bombed quickly down to about 15 metres, keeping a good hold on the buoy line. Greg held his camera up and ready with his right hand, floating outwards as he slid down the rope held with his left hand. I got behind the hawser, grasping it with both knees and fins, holding the older camera in front of the rope, with one arm around each side of the thick line.

We first saw the orcas about 15 to 20 metres away, and they were quickly closing on us. The front orca had a stingray clamped in its jaws, and it was twisting and turning its head as if it was showing off its catch. A calf was beneath it and a smaller adult on the offside. Greg let go of the rope, filming continuously, drifting with the flow of the tide. There was no way I was going to let go, and I became separated from Greg by about 3 metres; I started clicking on his old camera from behind the hawser.

A fourth orca, larger than any of the others, appeared out of the deeper gloom well below us and swept upwards heading straight for me, but when it saw the hawser, it veered away from me at the last possible instant. Briefly, I let go of the rope and recoiled back in horror as it scooped Greg up in its huge mouth, legs out one side and arms sticking out the other. The orca passed very close, spinning me backwards in the wake of its huge undulating tail.

When they were gone, I found I was still clicking the camera button—out of fear, nervousness, or some other instinct I don't fully understand. I found a grip on the rope again and pulled myself back up, surfacing without a decompression stop, and slithering into the safety of the rubber duck.

Searchers found no trace of Greg, and at the memorial service, members of his family said he loved diving so much it was the way he would have chosen to go. I did not share that view but nodded pleasantly in harmony, knowing that they would feel better for a while at least. The police and the coroner looked at my photos several times—they seemed morbidly entranced by them—and concluded that his death was 'misadventure'. I did agree with that view!

It was a moral judgment and out of respect for Greg that I never entered any of the photos in the Club's Underwater Section.

However, I did enter one in a National Geographic competition. It showed the big orca carrying Greg away, bathed in surrealistic sunlight, observed by its three companions, their eyes all pivoted backwards, watching the instant of the catch, one with the stingray still firmly clamped in its jaws.

I won $10,000 in cash and a thirty-day diving tour of the Caribbean.

OLD BLUE

AS THE FOUR-WHEEL-DRIVE towing the eight-metre fibreglass boat skidded to a halt outside the pub, the plume of dust whirled around the old man and the dog—just as the old Māori painfully hoisted himself up onto the single step of the pub's porch.

'Well, there's your one man and a dog,' said the driver

with a laugh. 'You said this place looked like it had a population of one man and a dog.'

'Not sure you could count either of them,' the other replied. 'To count them, they have to be alive, don't they?'

The old grey-haired dog, favouring his front left leg as well as the diagonally opposite rear right leg, coughed weakly from the ingested dust as he shuffled in the pub door after his master.

'You'd be chuffed with the fish, though. I told you the Coromandel's not fished out like the Hauraki Gulf,' said the driver, leaping out of the vehicle and brushing his trackies clean. He was the taller of the two with swept-back fair hair firmly held in place with hair gel.

'You're right about that … I've never seen so many snapper, and the big one is a beauty!' His mate was short, with an evenly tanned complexion from regular visits to a suntan clinic. He wore expensive sunnies, had a number two haircut and stubble to match. They both wore two-toned sneakers and sweatshirts with identical designer logos on one breast.

'Well, let's get rid of the salt with a quick beer and get on the road.'

'What is the time?' said the short one, then looking at his watch, added, '11.45, good timing! We can still get back to Auckland for dinner and drinks with the girls tonight.'

They went into the pub, where the old Māori was leaning on the scarred wooden bar with a handle of Waikato. They could see the dog sprawled out at the far end of the long, almost empty, public bar, beside a sizeable dust-covered window, already loudly snoring in the only patch of sunlight in the bar.

'What would you like, boys?' asked the owner of the establishment.

'Couple of cold lagers. Do you have Heineken?'

'Nah, Lion or Waikato.'

'Couple of Lion will have to do.'

'How'd ya fishing go?' asked the publican as he got their stubbies.

'Great! Got a bin of snapper, one massive one, out by the pinnacles.'

'No big fish left out there now,' said the old Māori. 'Used to catch big ones with a hand line—just out here in front of the pub. Even out by the pinnacles, there's no big fish left anymore.' He sipped on his handle of draft as the two young men glared at him.

'Do you want me to bring the bloody bin in to prove it,' asked the driver.

'Good idea,' said the publican. 'Prove your point, wouldn't it?'

The driver, visibly angry, left the bar to get the fish, and the short dark young man asked sarcastically, 'So you used to catch big ones yourself. Was that before or after the Second World War?'

'Both,' said the old man calmly, ignoring the rudeness.

'And was your old dog there too, as a witness?'

'Not then, only after the war. Saved my life once—old Blue—we were pig hunting—Blue came outa the bush on his own—fetched my cuz after a big tusker gored me leg.'

'Doesn't look much like a pig dog now, 'bout time he was put down by the look of him,' said the Aucklander.

'Blue's time is not up yet; he's still smarter than any man I've ever met,' said the old man affectionately.

The other Aucklander struggled in with his fish bin and dumped it on the floor beside the old man, who leaned over and looked at the fish with disgust.

'Would've kept that one,' he said, 'it's hardly big though—but the rest are just tiddlers.'

'They're all legal,' claimed the driver. 'We measured them.'

'Yeah, sure,' said the old Māori. 'But I would've still chucked them back. You Pakeha are why there are no big ones anymore.'

The two young men sipped their beer and glared at the old fellow who had nearly finished his handle of beer.

'He claimed his dog is smarter than either of you two,' said the publican, deliberately personalising the old man's earlier comment.

The old man looked down but remained silent.

'If you can prove that dog is smarter than me, you can have the big fish,' said the tall, fair yuppie, picking it up and slapping it on the bar in front of the old man.

The old man looked at them both and slowly nodded as if there was no doubt whatsoever about the point he had made —it was just a matter of how to prove it. In the silence that followed, the dog coughed, shuddered as if it was experiencing an old nightmare, and the snoring became even louder than before. The two young men smiled at each other and drained the last of their beers.

'Maybe I can prove it,' said the old man.

'Oh Yeah!' said the Aucklanders in unison.

'I reckon I can prove that Blue can read my mind, and you Pakeha couldn't do that, could you?'

The Aucklanders snorted their disbelief.

'Without saying a word, I will ask Blue to signal midday to us in some way. If he doesn't deliver, I'll get you both another beer.'

The barman immediately slapped two more stubbies beside the big fish.

'No whistling, finger-snapping, foot-tapping, or any other secret signals?' asked the tall one. 'No tricks?'

'No tricks, no nothin', I can't even see Blue from here,' replied the old man.

The Aucklanders looked at each other grinning: 'What the hell, you're on, but it has to be inside 15 seconds, either side of noon, on my Rolex,' said the short one.

'And you'll need to get on with it; you've only got 30 seconds to go,' he said, looking at his watch.

The old man nodded and put one hand over his eyes in deep concentration as if he was communicating subconsciously with his dog.

The short dark Aucklander quietly counted down intervals of five seconds before the hour, 'Twenty-five … twenty … fifteen … ten … five.'

The dog stirred in his corner, and his deep snoring seemed to stop.

The Aucklander grinned at his mate. 'Zero, we're halfway.'

The dog snuffled, stood up, thrust its head high up, and began howling like a wolf.

The old man drained his handle, politely thanked them for the fish, and picked it up by shoving one hand into a gill flap. The publican turned away to put the beer back in the cooler so that no one could see his beaming face. The old man walked to the door, the weight of the big fish causing him to lean the opposite way to stay on balance, and the dog followed in a similar wobbly gait. The dumbfounded Aucklanders stood at the bar, shocked to the core, unable to believe what they had witnessed, as their big fish disappeared out the door.

When the old man got across the road and inside the gate to his old whare, he leant over and patted his dog, 'I keep tellin' ya Blue, ya shouldn't worry about the mill's lunchtime siren.' The dog wagged its tail, its whole body shaking in harmony; the old man shook his head in wonder at how a dog could hear something so far away, well beyond any man's hearing.

DOLL FINN

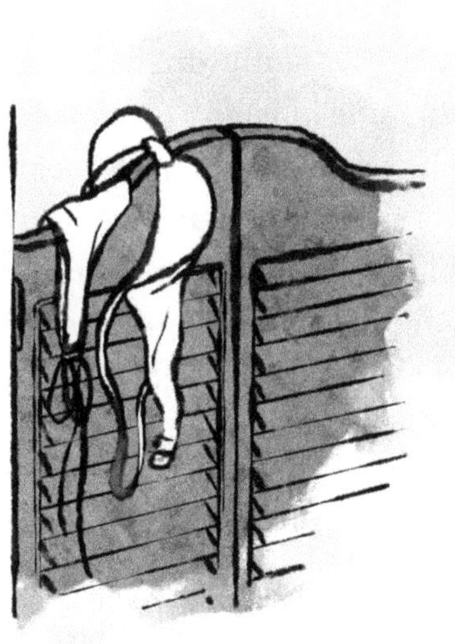

AS FAR AS I can remember, the skipper was the first who referred to Judith Finn as Doll Finn. He said it was natural enough to call a diver 'Dolphin' and, besides, she reminded him of Dolly Parton. She was undoubtedly a match in build for the busty singer, but that's where the resemblance ended. She did not have the smile or charm, let alone the voice, of Dolly Parton. When Doll opened her mouth, she was unmistakably Australian with a harsh nasal twang, an aggressive nature, and a vocabulary she could only have learnt in a woolshed, at the bottom of a rugby league maul, or somewhere even less reputable.

'What are you bloody jokers staring at?' she demanded as she emerged, vacuum-packed in her pink wetsuit. We all knew what we were staring at, alright, but not one of us dared to say. So we geared up in silence, looking at our feet, and making falsely polite conversation with one another. Doll Finn inverted her bottle and buoyancy compensator and flipped them over her head, macho-style. She straightened up and stretched to help her rig slide into position. My buddy, sneaking a glance, feared or hoped (I'm not sure which) that she would burst out of her tautly-strained neoprene suit.

We piled over the side in pairs, some going hunting, some taking photographs, and others just looking. Doll Finn followed a couple of the divers, watching them pluck crayfish from grooves and holes. Soon she had joined in, shoving her arm up crevices without any fear at all. My buddy and I went in the opposite direction, and I got a couple of crayfish myself, but my buddy chased an octopus around, putting it in the sugar bag he used for a catch bag. On the way back to the boat, it kept pushing tentacles out the top of the bag, and he kept pushing them back in. I don't know why he bothered keeping it; the damn thing was to prove to be more trouble than it was worth.

We got back to the boat, the skipper did a tally to make sure everyone was on board, and we exchanged stories of our dive. Doll joined in, saying how catching crayfish was great fun and a lot easier than she had thought it would be. You got used to her harsh voice after a while, and she began to relax, almost as if she felt she was one of the boys. We were all still pretty self-conscious in her presence because if there is one sure thing in this life, it was that she was not 'one of the boys'.

Some of us had a hot shower (the skipper said later it probably should have been a cold shower) and emerged from the light-louvred door onto the stern deck and changed as modestly as life on board allowed. Doll Finn stripped off her wetsuit in front of us and disappeared behind the bat-wing door in her bikini, which she removed and hung over the top of the door as she showered. The divers, all grown men, seemed to become little boys again and giggled and rolled their eyes while a gentle humming of contentment and happiness came from the shower, reminding us of what was behind the door.

It was no single person who thought of it or instigated it; it was more akin to the group action of a school of fish that inexplicably shifts in the sunlight, going from silver to blue and back to silver. Animal psychologists have all sorts of pet ideas about such group behaviour, some referring to the Phalanx Theory. They apply their various theories to flocks of migrating birds, herds of wildebeest, audiences at rock concerts, and even tracking people's walking patterns in supermarkets.

Some blamed the octopus for emerging from the sugar bag at that particular time. The skipper said my buddy should never have brought it back on board. I thought that Doll Finn should not have hung her bikini pieces over the door as if to taunt those on the deck outside.

Anyway, they started by grabbing a tentacle each and gently stretching the octopus between them in harmless play. The octi became a bit agitated, its eyes bulged in fear, and it changed from dull grey to vibrant maroon. They swung the poor beast back and forth a bit like a floppy skipping rope. My buddy said, 'one', but no one else said or did anything. Then, on the next swing, someone else said, 'one-two', but there was still no clear plan of action. When a third person said, 'one-two-three', we all knew what we were going to do even though no one had signalled it, and the octi went in over the top of the bat-wing door.

There was a surprisingly long pause, probably only a second or two, but it seemed a lot longer. It was as if, for a long instant, we did not throw the octi in there. Then there was a gasp, a scream, and a crash as Doll Finn entirely ignored the door's existence to exit the shower. The hinges and catch splintered away from the doorframe, and the door slammed, clattering on the deck. We all ran like kids caught stealing fruit as Doll Finn emerged into the sunlight wearing only an octopus.

HUNTER-GATHERER

THE TWINS WATCHED as he took the coffee to his wife, still warm in bed, and they followed him to the kitchen when he went to the fridge to get the sandwiches she had made for his day's fishing. He ate a couple of leftover cooked sausages and broke off a chunk of cheese to eat on the way. The twins even went out on the back porch and watched as he put his fishing gear in the ute: his rod and reel, bait and a new packet of hooks, and his jacket and lunch. The twin tabbies were quite different from each other. She was slim, had a pretty face, and walked in a dainty way; he was chunkier, quite ugly from his many scars, and he swaggered aggressively when he walked. They were tabbies from the same litter; their father was unknown and assumed to be one of the male cats from the hedge at the back house. Fiona named the female tortoiseshell Alexis who always came when her mistress called 'Lexie'. The male would only ever answer the deep, gruff call of 'Scruff!' from his master—the one he knew would bring fish home that night.

Lexie leapt up on the bed and curled up by her mistress while Scruff ate some of the chopped meat leftovers from the previous night. It had congealed and stuck to the dish, so he held the bowl with one paw and wrenched each piece free with his teeth before chewing and swallowing it. Lexie would only eat fresh meat, and it had to be finely chopped. She had eaten her small share the previous night, so Scruff now cleaned up the balance. He turned to the bowl of milk, set now like a junket, just the way he liked it, and in a business-like manner, he finished that too. After his breakfast, he went out through the cat door and headed for the front gate.

Fiona stroked Lexie, and Lexie purred. Fiona would drink her coffee and then get up. After a bit of a tidy up in the house, she would carry on sewing the curtains she had been working on each weekend. She didn't mind her husband fishing occasionally. He worked hard at his job as a foreman bricklayer, and she knew he had to handle difficult staff, one who argued all the time and another who was just plain lazy.

To get some staff to follow instructions, it took a physical confrontation on more than one occasion. She knew he was a hard man, capable of giving as well as receiving; the scar on his cheek was evidence of that. But he was also a fair man, and he was steadily doing up the house for her. His fishing mates were not all that wholesome, one had recently divorced, and some drank too much, but her husband told her booze and boats don't mix, and she found that reassuring.

At the ramp, the fishermen stowed their gear and launched the six-metre fibreglass boat, and as they left the harbour, they radioed the coastguard giving details of their plans for the day. As they put the boat up to planing speed, Scruff was swaggering down the street a couple of houses from the corner where he lived. He was going to sort out the ginger cat that had ambushed him and jagged a piece out of his right ear the previous week. After carefully peering around the corner, Scruff could see his foe curled up on the front porch like a guard that had gone to sleep on the job. Scruff may have swaggered when he walked, but he was like a panther when he ran: swift, focused, and onto Ginger without warning or mercy. So when the neighbours opened the front door to rescue Ginger, Scruff was swaggering out their front-drive, well satisfied with his results.

Fiona had vacuumed the house by the time the boat was anchored, and they had their hooks baited and their lines in the water. Lexie was shifting from room to room, finding a sunny spot, usually in Fiona's way, and getting shooed off, which they both enjoyed. Scruff had crossed the street corner diagonally and was sitting outside a brick house. Scruff knew it was Saturday, only he thought of it as Fish-day, and he expected the owner of the brick house to emerge soon because, wet or dry, he always took his dog for a walk on Fish-day. The cat was patient. He sat by the brick fence about the same time as the fishermen were catching their first fish. Earlier, he had heard the vacuum cleaner at his place, and now he could hear the faint buzz of the sewing machine. Scruff enjoyed the quietness of the street, away from washing machines, hair driers, and other domestic disturbances.

The sea was flat and tranquil, and the men were reef fishing for snapper, using a selection of hooks and baits. Those with small hooks were catching tarakihi, so those with larger sizes changed their hooks down a couple of sizes, and they caught some too. Pipis seemed to be more successful than anything else, so they shared that bait around. They threw the odd leather jacket they hooked in a bucket at the stern of the boat.

Finally, the dog towed his master out the gate. Scruff bristled and hissed, and the dog yelped in fear. 'Settle down,' said the man, 'It's only Scruff!' The dog did not share that simplistic viewpoint and dragged its owner out in a big arc, over the grass berm, across the street onto the footpath opposite, skirting around the cat. The cat shifted from its aggressive, arched stance to sitting on its haunches in grim satisfaction at letting the dog know who was in charge of that particular piece of territory. The man and dog moved further down the street, the man whistling out of tune and the dog looking back nervously.

Scruff ignored Fiona, calling him for lunch. She had a lettuce salad, and Lexie had a small portion of jelly meat from a can. At about the same time, in a peaceful secluded bay, the fishermen chatted about work and home as they ate their chunky sandwiches and bulging bread rolls and drank hot soup or coffee from a thermos. With a nice catch of tarakihi already in their bin, they decided to go out off the point for kingfish.

Meanwhile, Scruff noticed the open front door at the old

lady's house, walked in, quickly ate the can of sardines set out for her fat lazy Persian, and casually walked out the cat-door at the rear. He paused there on the back porch to wash the oily remnants from his whiskers. The old lady had picked up a broom, so he leapt from the top step of the porch onto the top of the wooden fence, checked the other side for safety, and dropped first onto the compost bin and then into the overgrown vegetable garden. From there, he made his way back home and curled up for a well-earned afternoon nap in his favourite spot in the back hedge.

When the fisherman returned home, Lexie was waiting in the front window—so was Fiona, but Scruff was nowhere to be seen. The men had filleted their tarakihi on the boat, and Fiona crumbed some fillets while her husband had a cold beer and stripped the skin from the leather jackets, like pulling vinyl off an old cupboard shelf. Lexie brushed around her legs while Fiona took some trimmings of the fish and lightly cooked the small pieces in the pan while it heated up for the tarakihi fillets. She put the warm fish in the cat's bowl, and Lexie purred as she ate it.

'Where's Scruff?' asked the fisherman.

'I don't know. He went out first thing, and I haven't seen him since. The people two houses down complained about him again. They said they had to take their moggy to the vet.'

The fisherman laughed and went out on the back porch and called out 'Scruff!' Before long, the cat swaggered in from the back hedge and began gnawing on the tough, raw flesh of a leather jacket.

HARD-LUCK HARRY

I HAD KNOWN Harry from schooldays—we had always been best mates. He was a fine fellow: a good family man, a hard worker, and always helped his friends. But he was the unluckiest man I ever met. He sold his house on the corner of the main road, and the new owner sold it a couple of years later at a huge profit to a developer who built a new petrol station. When he did buy an investment property, the guts dropped out of the market, and he nearly lost his new house.

His worst luck, though, was in fishing. He had been a foundation member of the game fishing club and over the years held most of the committee positions: president, treasurer, club captain, and so on. He always worked hard on the committee, without any fanfare, almost anonymously. Being handy with a welder, he had even built the weighing gantry for the fish when the club first started up. His ambition was to catch a marlin, and I know he often pictured himself at the weigh station with his big rod and an even bigger smile, posing by his big catch.

He got the prize for the biggest snapper one year, the most species another, and he had caught many big kingfish. But he had never landed a marlin! As he grew older, he became quite bitter about his lack of luck with marlin, and it never helped when at every tournament prize-giving, his friends rubbed it in. He said to me once, 'Success is getting what you want in life, and based on my ambition to catch a marlin, I'm a failure, and everyone knows it.'

I don't think it pays to tell people what you want: it can jinx it ever happening. Harry hadn't been feeling well, and he missed meeting me for a beer and a smoke one Friday night, so I called around at his house the next day to see how he was. He had just had a medical check-up, and he told me the bad news.

'I'm riddled with cancer and have only a few weeks to live.'

Talk about bad luck! I didn't know what to say, so I said nothing.

'Fair mind to get it over with now,' he said.

'Don't do that,' I said, 'the classic is on next weekend. You'll get one last chance to catch your marlin.'

'The trouble is,' said Harry, 'I have a term life policy, and if I die after the end of the month, Gloria will get nothing because the ten-year term of my policy will be up. If I do myself in now, at least I will have paid the mortgage off for Gloria. I'd have to do it secretly, though, because suicide would probably invalidate my policy.'

As I said earlier, he wasn't the luckiest man I ever met; one bit of bad news always seemed to be followed by a worse bit.

'Maybe you'll get lucky,' I told him. What else could I say?

Harry seemed determined to kill himself for the insurance money, but he reluctantly agreed to my suggestion to delay his rather ghastly plan until after the fishing tournament. There would still be a few days left before the end of the month. I hoped that by then, he would have changed his mind.

Luck has a strange way of intervening in our lives. Harry struck his marlin late on the last day of the three-day classic. He worked it carefully and skillfully, as he had seen so many others do over the years. He seemed determined to put aside his ill health for as long as it took. We got it alongside. It was no record breaker—only a blue marlin and less than 100 kilograms—but it was a marlin! He was exhausted from his illness and the effort landing the marlin, but the smile did not leave his face from the instant we had it on board. I knew he was picturing himself at the weigh station that he had built for his marlin.

We flew the marlin flag, blue on white, all the way back, and the radio waves went wild, 'Old Harry has got his marlin at last!' We chalked up his name and the boat name, and the modest weight of the big fish on the blackboard and Harry stood alongside it beaming from ear to ear as the cameras flashed and all his mates cheered. He did not hear the wrenching of the fatigued steel on the top of the 20-year old gantry because he was so entranced with his catch. Everyone else leapt clear, but the dead fish spun around, knocking Harry into the water. The twisting of the fish and the impact hitting Harry broke the weld right off; the fish followed Harry into the water, driving him down to the bottom onto the sand.

Several younger guys jumped in to help old Harry, but the marlin's bill had pierced his chest, pinning him there, the fish standing vertically, swaying in the gently moving tide. Eventually, we got a diver to put a noose around the fish's tail, and we dragged it back up. By then, though, Harry was dead, either from drowning or from the terrible chest wound —certainly not from cancer—or suicide.

Everyone—except me—thought it strange that as they lifted Harry from the water and laid him out on the jetty, he was still smiling.

SHARK ATTACK

MANY EVENTS in life occur when some unexpected incremental factor adds to some already known dangers. The victim may, with reasonable care, have expected to control their destiny, but that small extra factor determines their fate. A hasty driver, pushing his ability to the limit, will cause a tragedy when a kid chases a ball onto the street. Or a young fellow will crash his car when a pretty blonde walks past. Pretty blondes have been the extra factor in many a man's fate.

Two of my scuba diving mates, a father and son, both called Sam, invited disaster into their lives. The father, a steady, relaxed guy with greying hair, a little jowly, a little paunchy. So that each Sam would know who I was speaking to, I began calling him Flotsam a few years back. His son, fitter, quicker and a lot more impetuous, I called Jetsam. The nicknames stuck, probably because they were well suited, and even the woman who was married to one Sam and the mother to the other occasionally referred to them as Flotsam and Jetsam.

Mostly, they always dived together, so each instinctively understood what the other thought and could respond quickly in an emergency.

They were diving off the Coromandel coast, near Castle Rock, on a pinnacle that started 30 metres below the surface and bottomed out to a sandy floor at 50 metres. Usually, they got their crayfish quota well before they reached the bottom, but on this day, there was less lobster than usual near the top of the pinnacle. Besides, Flotsam had speared a couple of john dory circling the pinnacle, using a short Hawaiian sling he carried with him, not a recommended practice while on scuba. He pushed the bleeding, quivering fish into his catch bag, attached to his weight belt with a brass spring clip, and they descended further down the pinnacle after their targeted prey, the spiny red lobster, or crayfish.

The three-metre mako shark was aware there were divers in the water from more than a kilometre away, recognising their characteristic clumsy vibrations and noises. Although he had not eaten for more than 30 hours after an unsuccessful excursion for food further out in deep blue water, he had little interest in humans as prey. A man's unfamiliar body heat, strange non-fish odours, and their inanimate and inedible equipment covering their bodies had no appeal. So he instinctively avoided these unusual beasts. He occasionally took a fish from a float on a line towed by such a creature but resisted any temptation to attack the man as it awkwardly flapped its way across the surface.

However, the distress signal of one john dory, followed almost immediately by a second, caused the mako to turn towards the activity, but he did so cautiously. Flotsam and Jetsam, oblivious of the approaching danger, plunged downwards, and the deeper they went, the bigger the crayfish. So they left the smaller ones and focused on wrenching the larger ones from the slots and overhangs on the pinnacle. By the time they bottomed out close to 50 metres deep, each had their legal limit of six crayfish, all generous in size. They were deeper than was safe for any prolonged length of time, and Flotsam pointed upwards with one hand, inflating his buoyancy compensator with the other, and Jetsam nodded his assent.

They still had plenty of air in their tanks to make a lengthy recompression stop on the anchor rope. This action would avoid excessive nitrogen absorbed into their bloodstream bubbling out like champagne bubbles as they ascended, putting them at risk. Their dive computers told them they had been too deep too long and would need to stop for at least eight minutes at five metres deep to get out of the red zone. Their computers immediately indicated they were ascending a little too quickly, so they carefully dumped a little air from their buoyancy vests to slow their upward progress. As the beeping of their computers stopped, it took no more than a meeting of their eyes to acknowledge this precautionary move. They were always cautious about ascending too quickly.

As they found the anchor rope at about 15 metres, Jetsam's quick eye first saw the slowly circling shark, unaware it had been following them up from the deep. It was 20 metres away, just at the limit of their visibility in the cloudy conditions under the water. Flotsam, seeing and sensing the fear in his son, followed his moving line of vision and saw the heavily-built beast circling them, its slowly undulating tail smooth and rhythmic. Jetsam pointed at the blood still trickling from his father's catch bag attached to his weight belt. Flotsam nodded and plunged his arm in among the crayfish to extract and dump the two dead john dory.

The shark could smell the fish blood and sense their final flutterings of life but could not see the fish. There was no trailing line, distant from the men, holding the fish—only the men themselves, and the smell and vibrations seemed to emanate from the men, mixed with their emissions of heat and human odours. He circled closer, and as he did so, the swaying of his tail became more rapid, his primal instincts pushing up the rate of his heartbeat. His pectoral fins pressed downwards to control his body movements, and his eyes, hard and black, like glowing embers, focussed on his potential prey. As the shark turned and weaved, its eyes never left the men. It circled over them, swam under them and around them, closer and closer, searching for the source of fish blood.

Flotsam could not separate the fish from among the cluster of crayfish that pressed down upon them, gripping each other and the fish into a hard ball. He handed the small spear to Jetsam so he could use both hands to get at the fish.

He could touch them but not free them from the grip of the crayfish.

The mako was now in a frenzy, moving in violent twitching movements, almost brushing against the men. Its circles had tightened, and it had now identified which of the two creatures was fish and which was man. To the shark, as it flashed to and fro in front of Flotsam, the man was fish, and the fish was man. Jetsam was irrelevant.

Flotsam gave up trying to free the fish and desperately sought to release his catch bag clipped to his weight belt, hoping the excited mako would follow the catch bag containing the fish downwards. He fumbled for the brass clip as the shark turned and started its run, like a bull in an arena on the charge. Both men knew there was no time to free the bag as the dark, glittering eyes and grim wide mouth headed straight for Flotsam at chest height.

The jaws opened, exposing the inch-long teeth, sharp and sloping back inwards, to assist the tearing of flesh from its prey. As the shark's jaw hinged backwards to make its attack, Jetsam released the rubber on the sling, and the short three-pronged spear impaled itself in the back of the shark's throat. The shark reared up and turned aside as the men recoiled backwards. The slashing tail smashed Flotsam's mask, brushing the mouthpiece away from his face, and thrusting him back against Jetsam.

The younger man had an instant recollection of a circus where he had seen a lion tamer thrust his chair at a lion. He wondered if the shark would attempt to wreak its revenge upon him, just as the snarling lion had threatened to attack the trainer. He discounted that possibility as he saw the shark disappearing into the gloom, with a gush of blood streaming behind it and with the spear still sticking from its throat.

His father had grabbed the anchor rope again and tried to

recover his mouthpiece as Jetsam recovered his senses and went to help him. Flotsam had bitten through the silicone of his mouthpiece, rendering it useless, and Jetsam took a couple of deep breaths of air and thrust his mouthpiece in his father's mouth. As they hung on the anchor rope, sharing the mouthpiece during their recompression stop, they both pondered that extra factor that almost determined their fate.

Perhaps the mako was having similar thoughts.

BIG MAN SMALL MAN

OFTEN WE WOULD SEE them together, on their boss's boat or at one of the leaners in a Whakatane bar, and we would laugh just at the sight of them because one was nearly two metres high while the other was a little over five feet.

Nobody ever used their proper names. The big guy was called Lofty, and the little guy they called Devito. He looked and behaved like a young Danny Devito.

If there was any raucous behaviour in the bar, Devito was always at the centre of it; if there was a quarrel on a boat, he was generally there causing it. He seemed to make up for his lack of size with his hyperactivity. But he was a crafty little sod, savvy about the law, and if there was any trouble, he always came out as clean as a Teflon-coated pan. Lofty, on the other hand, because he was so big and dumb, got blamed for everything, even if he was not involved. He got kicked out of pubs and clubs because he was so visible. If anyone threatened Devito or his boss, Lofty would step forward. Not that he ever had to do anything. His size, booming voice and massive fists were sufficient deterrent. The fact was, though, he had never hurt anyone in his life. Whenever the cops arrived, they immediately saw him as a challenge, and Lofty got frog-marched out as an example to everyone else.

Their boss, Harvey, traded in powerboats but sold a bit of pot and sometimes cocaine, ecstasy or other stuff on the side. Well, we all knew he didn't exactly sell it so much as 'spec' it for a commission, putting buyer and seller into contact. He kept clear of problems with the law because he never personally handled the money or the drugs and was careful about any loose talk in bars or on the phone. His caution paid off because, when there was a big drug bust a couple of months earlier, the cops did not even question him. Nevertheless, since then, he had been doubly careful, laying low until things calmed down again.

Harvey was an interesting character, a bit on the tubby side for a man in his mid-thirties, with closely cropped dark hair. He had excellent contacts with some very naughty girls who would always turn up when he and his mates wanted to party. Life had been pretty good for him and his two contrasting employees, Lofty and Devito. Lofty cleaned the boats and did all the dirty work while Devito kept radios, depth sounders, and other bits and pieces going long enough for Harvey to make a quick sale at a good profit. He did not pay them much, but they would party at Harvey's expense after a good week. The food, the booze, the girls and anything else they wanted coming as a tax-free bonus.

But Harvey had a spot of bad luck. One of the big Volvos on his floating gin palace seized up! When the diesel mechanic pulled the engine out, they test-ran the other one and told him that it would blow up too if he kept using it. So he was up for two reconditioning jobs on his boat engines which made him very angry. He usually on-sold any boat before it needed any expensive work, but he had kept this one a little too long.

Harvey's business that year had been quieter than usual. He had ground rent to pay at the boatyard, his monthly 'floor plan' payment to the company financing his boat stock, and wages for Lofty and Devito. Things were pretty tough right then for Harvey; he was a bit stretched at the bank and needed to get his boat back in the water for the big fishing tournament. He knew that he would have to go on the long waiting list to enter in future years if he did not participate.

Harvey also had his pride: there was no way he would leave his boat laid up until he could afford the repairs, so he told the mechanic to go ahead and do up both engines. He was confident the cost of $20,000 would show up one way or another. If it came to a pinch, he could add a few non-existent 'ghost' boats to his floor plan and add the extra money to his debt with the finance company. He had done that and repaid the money a few times before the finance company had done one of their random checks. But never for such a large amount, and it made him furious to think about needing to use that ploy. After all, it was still debt he had to repay at some time.

His anger and bad luck seem to go in harness, one feeding off the other, just as sometimes his good trading and good luck seem to be mutual attractants, leading to good deals. Harvey became furious when the diesel mechanic told him his engines were worse than expected because sand was in the engine oil. Their estimate for repairs was up another $10,000. He received this news the same day as the finance company made a spot check on the boats in his yard, closing off that option for paying for the repairs.

Coincidence or otherwise, he received a visit from one of his business contacts who needed his help the next day. He had a yacht arriving from Southeast Asia with some bundles on board, and he needed them picked up before the vessel made landfall. Harvey would not have customarily touched the job, having turned down the same contact for similar jobs in the past, but he knew the diesel mechanic would insist on a cheque to complete the engine repairs.

Harvey decided he would do it this one time and told the man he wanted $60,000. Eventually, he got an agreement for $50,000, cash on delivery, for the one night's work. The job was planned for late Saturday night because, his contact said, 'Even the cops have got to party some time!' Harvey's luck was returning because he could give the mechanic a cheque on Saturday morning, and that would not clear until Monday, by which time he would have their $30,000 covered and $20,000 for himself. A bonus would be running in the engines a week before the fishing tournament.

So, Harvey, Lofty and Devito set off for a midnight rendezvous, 50 kilometres out, beyond Mayor and White Islands, setting their GPS to the coordinates given by the contact. Harvey took care to keep the revs of his reconditioned diesel engines at the level recommended by the mechanic. The yacht they met was a seventy-footer, fitted out for bluewater sailing, showing just a night-light as she rolled without mooring in the gentle swell. A lookout waved Harvey alongside, and the delivery was planned to be quick and made with little exchange of words.

In heavy jackets and hoods, the yachtsmen waited for the right roll of both boats and threw ten large bails and six smaller bundles down onto the power boat's stern deck. The yacht chugged off into the gloom to make its late afternoon arrival in Auckland the next day while Harvey and his odd-ball crew stowed the bails below and turned back towards Whakatane to make their rendezvous with his contact at the jetty.

They had a few rums on the way back to warm up and were feeling good as they pulled into the jetty berth. Devito used the boat hook to lift the mooring ropes, and Lofty pulled the boat across to loop each rope over a bollard. After the boat was secure, Harvey shut the smoothly purring engines down. In the silence, disturbed only by lapping water, ten armed police from the drug squad, looking like ghostly apparitions, arose all around them and swarmed aboard.

It was only when he was shackled in the van that Harvey realised it was all a police setup. From coinciding their scam with the fishing tournament, to the sand in his engine oil, and his finance company's inspection of his boatyard. Beneath his breath, Harvey kept mumbling, over and over, 'It was all a setup. Fuck the police!'

THE DIVER

'LAST DAY, LAST DIVE, LAST CHANCE,' I said, watching Donnie pull on his wetsuit.

'That's right. I'm gonna test myself on this one—like I've never done before. I'm going down the dropoff to get a big one.'

The others looked up from their preparation for their wreck dive.

'You know our rule,' I said. 'Twenty metres for twenty minutes.'

'Yep, or 200 metres forever!' Donnie replied, using one of our old jokes, only his face was serious. The skipper and other divers on board laughed. Our black humour applied to the use of scuba gear when today we were freediving, but it was still a dive-safe message everyone understood. We would be using a wetsuit, weight belt, fins, mask and snorkel—no air bottle or buoyancy compensator like the others.

Donnie gave me a wink and a grin as we finished gearing up, and the skipper took us to the seaward face at the north end of the island. Before we jumped over the side, he carefully confirmed our plans: 'You're going down the inside face of the island, and we'll see you both at the south end in an hour and a half or so, two hours at the most?' We acknowledged this by making a circle with thumb and forefinger.

There was a light breeze from north to south that would make our two- to three-kilometre traverse of the island a leisurely swim. We rolled overboard into about eight metres of water. The visibility was good. There were big boulders below us, and we paddled over patches of green and brown kelp towards the top end of the island. We could see that it was low tide because the boulders above the surface were still wet from the earlier high tide. When the tide turned, we knew there would be a slight undertow towards the mainland that lay about five kilometres to the west. Our shadows caused the crabs and demoiselles to scatter for cover, but soon we had passed over the shallows, and the ocean floor sloped away to deeper water. Here, our view downwards was a hemisphere of a thirty-metre radius, but we could only see the front half of the hemisphere unless we looked back. Below us, we could see red moki, angelfish and a few leatherjackets, hovering like army helicopters. The depths beyond were a deep iridescent blue: mysteriously dangerous, magically attractive.

Glancing up, we could see the mainland but, because of the earth's curvature and the slight chop, we could not see the shoreline or the dunes. It was a barren part of the coast inaccessible by car. The hills were dark in the shade of the late afternoon sun, and the trampers' track just a pencil line through the dark trees, a charcoal sketch, untouchable and distant. The boulders and island were behind us now, and I stopped. I lifted my mask, and Donnie did the same. 'We part company here, I think.'

'Yep,' Donnie said. 'I'm goin' wider out to the deeper water, and you're goin' down the inner face to burley up in the shallows.'

'Take care,' I said.

'Sure! You too! Remember, you'll see me down the south end about ten minutes before the boat arrives. And maybe during your dive, you'll get a few glimpses of my fins as I go up and down.' Donnie had always been a crafty guy.

'Hah! Sure thing,' I said, and we high-fived.

I watched him replace his mask and snorkel and flick his fins to surge away. He was a faster swimmer than me—slim, agile and smooth. His three-quarter-metre fins matched his build, so there was little wasted energy. I was a slow, awkward clunker in comparison.

He disappeared behind the first swell and, as I turned back towards the island, it was against the light pull of the turning tide. As I finned forward, I armed my speargun, pulling the rubber back to the top notch. I freed up the trailing line so that the float I was towing moved further back to about thirty metres behind me, its torpedo shape offering little resistance. The bottom soon became visible again. As I had expected, the exposed boulders were covered with kina, hundreds of look-alike hedgehogs exposing themselves to currents from which they fed—and divers who smashed them up to create a feeding frenzy of fish. The conditions were perfect. I hoped they suited Donnie as well.

About twenty metres from the face of the island, I swung south towards a protruding reef where water was breaking over rocks that stood in the face of the light swell. The reef was no more than an extension of one of the many bush-covered ridges on the island. Each pair of ridges created a little bay, and in the first bay, I could see a colony of shags with the tell-tale white signs of their accumulated shit covering the branches and leaves of two or three intertwined pohutukawa.

I worried about Donnie in the open water, but then I had always worried about Donnie. Even at college, I had worried about him: sharp as a knife with his mouth, but pretty dumb in class; quick as a flash as a flanker, but a bit quick with his fist in a ruck. Hah! I suppose there's not much difference between detention and the sin bin!

My reverie vanished as I was distracted by movement on my right. I braced myself and lifted my gun as a school of a dozen kingies came in, charging towards me. They were big, of legal size, and I wanted to shoot a kingfish today, but I relaxed because it was too early in my dive. I would have to tow the bugger around for a couple of hours. They swept by, having a good look at me from a safe distance before turning back out to sea, their awesome power emphasised by the slow, rhythmic movement of their whole bodies.

I skirted the end of the reef and found a few blue maomao. I shot one that weighed about a kilo, but it was a body shot. My float had drifted in behind me. I removed the flapping fish from the spear by folding in the collapsible spear flaps and shoved the stainless spike attached to my float in one eye of the fish and out the other. The fish slid past the spike onto the wire. It was no longer struggling. The killing of one maomao attracted many more; the six became sixty, and I shot two more in quick succession, both nearer two kilos, both headshots. Hundreds of maomao now surrounded me, in lemming-like suicide, as if it was a privilege to join their mates on my spike. I shot four more and then discarded the small one shot through both fillets.

Donnie had once asked, 'How come you always shoot maomao in sets of three?'

'Hah!' I replied. 'I take the fillets from three fish to the fish shop, and I get six pieces of battered fish and a scoop of chips for under ten bucks: three for me, two for Lynley and one for Tigger.'

I moved around the face of the first bay. There were tens of thousands of tiny smelt in the calmer water, and shags were in the water duck-diving for them, often staying down and chasing the little fish until they got one. Just like me, I thought: get a good feed first, then go for a better one. The sun was still above the mainland hills, but its lower angle lit up the tiny fish swimming in and around the pastel-shaded kelp. Variegated rocks, rumbled smooth by time, covered the floor. I relaxed, enjoying my slow swim across the bay, wondering how Donnie was managing.

Donnie hadn't been long out of school before he experienced the occasional period of more severe detention, sometimes to detox, sometimes for assault, once for resisting arrest.

'I've always been a target,' he claimed.

When I said, 'Keep your head down … stop making yourself a bloody target,' he just laughed and shrugged. He never changed much over the years.

As I swam wide to pass the next rocky point, a gannet

with its wings folded inwards like a fighter plane on an aircraft carrier plunged from the sky. It rocketed into the water close beside me, the reverse of a Polaris missile, leaving a trail of entrapped air streaming upwards in its path. It scared the shit out of me, but after about ten seconds, it turned upwards with a trevally in its beak. Jeez! That's nearly a legal fish, I thought, longer than my maomao. I watched the bird take off, vigorously flapping its way up to speed until it could use its feet on the water to help its lift-off. Then, free of the water's resistance, it soared above the sea and headed towards the cliffs.

I was nearing my favourite spot—Spearo's Paradise, I call it—a set of pinnacles that came up from about thirty metres. Above them was an extensive green kelp forest at about twenty metres, and beside and above the kelp a boulder-strewn basin about ten metres deep, loaded with thousands of kina. The key feature was a rock ledge on the shoreward side of the basin with a deep trench behind it, a concealed path of approach for a cunning spearo, and along the ridge were a few scrawny brown kelp trees that swayed in the swell. I loved this place.

I let my speargun drop down into the trench from the surface, the yellow line tracking back up to the orange float holding the six maomao, their iridescence now faded to a paler blue. I removed a one-kilo weight from my weight belt and breathed up three or four times before plunging down into the boulder basin, where I began smashing kina with the lead weight. On each dive—and I did five dives in quick succession—I counted twenty smashed kina before resurfacing. Leatherjackets and parrotfish swarmed in to feast; sweep and maomao joined them, and the finer particles of blood and guts lifted in the swell and fell like a light mist onto the kelp forest on the lower level. It could not have been better. I had set the trap. I checked my watch, deciding to give it fifteen minutes before I returned, but as I retrieved my gun, a John Dory, attracted by the activity I had created, approached the melee below. I sunk into the trench, finned along to the centre point of the trap, emerging between two kelp bushes, and I shot the dory. He joined the maomao on the spike; the round black patch on his white side was the inviting target, and I had scored a bullseye.

I swam well away from my trap, resisting the temptation to check it out too soon. The bigger fish wait and watch, often circling beyond a diver's view, their silver scales making them almost transparent. I had wondered why the small fish didn't clean out all the food, but some of the kinas remain trapped in large pieces of their shells, and big snapper can crunch that stuff up and still get a feed after they know it's safe.

The police had set a trap too. An undercover cop had tried to buy some kiwi-green from Donnie, but he had only ever smoked the odd joint, never sold the stuff. Hell, I was as guilty as Donnie on that score! But Donnie—the bloody fool—bought into it. Not only that, but the next time the cop asked Donnie if he could source some cocaine for him as well. Well, why wouldn't he? He turned a quick buck the first time around; this would be even better and easier with someone he knew he could trust. Yeah right! Like two years better, and out after one.

When I returned to my rock basin, I did so underwater, silently and secretly along the trench, and I slid my speargun up between the swaying kelp branches before I could see over the ledge, finger already on the trigger. There were two big snapper, heads down, gutsing on the burley. I pulled the trigger as I adjusted my aim at the closest, only two metres from the point of the spear. It jerked as the spear hit, and the second fish shot out of the basin and vanished into the kelp forest. The speared fish shuddered and sought refuge under a boulder. I followed my line and spear shaft and seized the fish by its gill plate. I let the shaft go and removed my dive knife, inserted it between its eyes and shoved the blade in. My heart was beating hard, and I needed air, but I swam upwards slowly, maintaining my gloved grip on the fish's gills; the spear shaft and gun followed me up. As I gasped in some air, I towed the fish to the float and secured it on the spike before removing the spear. I was breathing heavily, and my heart was still racing as I released the now-secured fish and paddled away from my bleeding prey. It was a good fish, although I knew the other was even bigger. I could have waited to see if the other returned, but that was unlikely. That fish would be wiser for its experience, and I was happy with a fish I knew was seven or eight kilos. My breathing and pulse had steadied, and I moved forward again, feeling the extra drag of the snapper on my float, reducing my speed a little.

Donnie is the kinda guy that plays double or quits. He told me he'd not wasted his time on the inside. For the first time in his life, he'd paid attention in class, but he was at the University of Hard Knocks, and the tutors were hardened crims. I didn't see much of him for a while; he was all around the show, doing stuff I didn't want to know about. When the cops got him the second time, somehow, he got bail. We had a few chats over a beer or two, and we did some dives together, just like the old days. He was terrified and said he would rather die than go back inside.

'Some of them called me Pretty Boy,' he had said.

'Shit!' I'd replied.

I was approaching the south end of the island now, and ahead I could see the water breaking on Big Beast Point, a bit of a misnomer because I had never speared much just here, but we'd seen the odd bronze whaler snooping around the fish on our spikes. If you didn't keep an eye on them, they would steal your fish, sometimes cunningly chomping them off the wire without you noticing, sometimes taking them in a frenzied attack. They would cruise up from the deep next to the dropoff, a deep-water trench that ran the length of the island, where Donnie had said he intended to go down the face for some big crays.

Today, though, was quite different. As I reached the open water, another school of kingies came in, many more than I had seen earlier, maybe thirty or forty, and I checked behind me that my line was trailing freely. I did not want my fin or leg caught in a loop of the thick nylon cord. Be patient, I said to myself. I wanted a kill shot just behind the gills and through the spine. I chose my fish—not the closest, but moving into my target zone; not the biggest, but the best chance. The point of my spear swung in time with the movement of the fish. He U-turned in my face. Big mistake! Twang! The spear penetrated the fish at the perfect spot.

For a full second, nothing happened.

Then the school of big fish broke like a starburst, exploding in every direction, vanishing from sight. My fish, stunned, dipped his nose and fell deeper, but I knew more was to come. As he sank, I allowed him to take down the speargun attached by a nylon line to the spear; then, I paid out the thick cord that connected the butt of the speargun to the float—but only slowly. The fish now swam in a slow circle about twenty metres below me, and I firmed up my gloved hands on the cord, wrapping it once around my palms but in such a way that I could release it and payout more line. The fish burst back into life but was confined by the line; he first accelerated around the circle, then tested what was holding him by going straight down. I went with him, paying out a little more line but restricting him. He eased up and, as I floated back up to get a breath, I kept the pressure on the fish. He charged down several more times, each time a little weaker. When he began swimming in circles again, although he was deeper and the circles were bigger, I knew I had him. I just had to wait.

I star-fished on the surface, waiting and watching. He looked to be about twenty-five kilos, a nice fish. I was relaxed and breathing easy and in no hurry to transfer him to my spike. Hah! The longer I waited, the deader he got. A few minutes later, I heard the boat approaching. I looked at my watch—right on time. I looked at the mainland hills—the sun was right on the horizon, and the hills had become a blank canvas.

I knew Donnie would have retrieved his running gear by now and be halfway up the track. Tomorrow about noon, he would be in Sydney after using a passport he acquired with his cousin's licence and preparing to hitchhike to Perth. By then, with my assistance, the police divers would have just started their search.

SALMONELLA

BETWEEN THE RAKAIA and Rangitata Rivers in Mid-Canterbury is the Rangikura, a smaller, less-known stream that attracts salmon whose guidance system seems to have directed them between the two larger rivers. My theory is that the fish that attempt to migrate to the Rangikura's headwaters for spawning in spring are the progeny of one parent from each of the other two rivers. As a result, they appear to have averaged their destination. The cause is irrelevant; the effect, though is not, resulting in a proliferation of migrating fish in the mouth of the Rangikura.

However, difficulties arise fishing that river, the first being that there is no road to the mouth of the Rangikura. Nor is there beach access because the Rangikura empties into the Whakakiwi Bay that has impassable bluffs at each end. Some boats have come to grief attempting to navigate the river mouth because of the shifting sandbar and many small, sharp rocks below the surface. Land access is blocked on one side by a hapu who have not yet forgotten what happened in the sixties, the land frauds of the 1860s, that is. The other side of the river is farmed by a stud breeder who claims descent from an English feudal lord. He has threatened to have any 'poacher' sent to the penal colonies in Australia. That fate is hardly appealing. These difficulties in getting to the fishing zone mean, of course, that there is very little population pressure to deplete the fish numbers.

When I heard that old 'Lord' Algernon was laid up and hadn't been seen about for a while, I thought I would take my chance across the stud farm. His farm was on the south side of the mouth, which is usually better for salmon. I dismissed crossing the Māori land on the north face because they still had an old whalers' pot near the marae. My imagination was sufficient to deter me from testing the silly suggestions about how they may have previously used the pot.

My plan had one fundamental flaw: Algy was laid up alright—with his new, young wife, Ella, and she was something else! She had her eye on the main chance of a considerable inheritance and was not about to allow any depletion of her rights: financial, agricultural, riparian, or marital. Some said her excess exercise of the last-named right with poor old Algy might accelerate her inheritance of the other three. All flawed plans seem to attract other problems; that was how it seemed to me afterwards anyway.

I travelled light and alone: trackies, sneakers, a thick warm jersey for the coldness before dawn, my 3.6-metre surfcasting rod dismantled into three pieces, and a shoulder bag with my free-spool reel, various lures, a light parka, a stainless thermos of coffee, and a few sandwiches. I parked my old ute a little way up the road from the big homestead and, ignoring the trespass signs, headed across the paddocks to the mouth of the Rangikura River. That part of my excursion went well. The sheep I saw looked decidedly high class, a roll of wool around their throat like a fur stole, and those few that got up from the grass as I passed strutted arrogantly about as if they owned the place. The last paddock seemed empty except for one old ram in the far corner. I arrived at the mouth just as the sun emerged over the misty Pacific. I had a coffee and sandwich and carefully reconnoitred the situation.

There was little wind, the sea was flat, there was an outgoing tide which is when the salmon prefer to enter the river, and it was first light, their feeding time. I knew that fishermen would be shoulder to shoulder on every other river, but I had the whole river mouth to myself here. I positioned myself behind the single pine tree that blocked any view of the river mouth from the farm buildings, and there was no sign of life across the river at the marae. So I immediately set up my rod, fixed the reel, and selected a 60-gram, bright, stainless, ticer lure with two narrow strips of yellow fluorescent tape to increase my chances of attracting a strike. There was no fence to the paddock directly behind me, and I put my pack against an old tree stump. No Queen's chain was recognised here by either the Māoris or Lord and Lady Algernon!

My first cast was perfect, straight into the deep gut where the stream met the sea, and I slowly retrieved line with the drag locked up. At the first resistance to my gentle reeling, which was almost immediate, I struck the hook home and eased the drag tension to a fraction of the 10 kg breaking strain. I reeled it in, speeding up on each inward surge of the swell and easing off on the outward. The fish ran the line out a few times, but after only token resistance, I recovered the silver-iridescent salmon, used my sharp knife as an iki spike to put it out of its misery, and placed it in my tucker bag. I thought the beautifully conditioned fish would weigh around 10 kg.

The gut must have been a gathering place for that morning's inward migration because I caught my second and third fish similarly, each soon after its predecessor. At 10 kg each, I thought I already had enough weight to carry out and decided to call it a day when I noticed some residents of the marae across the other side of the river mouth, setting up their rods. They waved out in a friendly manner, and I waved back. I thought that if I left immediately after their arrival, I would arouse their suspicion, and they might contact my hostile unknowing hosts, Lord and Lady Algernon.

So I prepared for one last cast, seeking to make it an impressive throw, seeing as I now had an audience. I flicked the lure out behind me and, in one smooth motion, cast outwards towards the gut. Unfortunately, the single sheep in the paddock, a prize ram with twin curled horns, had moved up behind me to watch me cast. The trace wrapped itself twice around one horn and, as the unfortunate beast backed off in shock, the lure fixed itself firmly in one ear.

I know now that I should have immediately cut the line and walked away from that place, but I would not have been there in the first place if I was not one to take up a challenge. So I turned to face my quarry, gradually increased the drag, and slowly arrested the run of my trophy catch. The Māori spectators from across the river offered considerable encouragement, such as 'Great cast bro!' and 'Yeehaa!' This fish was neither frightened nor stupid. After being reluctantly reeled in, the ram decided that attack was the best form of defence. It came in at a brisk trot at first, then sped up to quick charging speed, far faster than I could reel in the line, faster even than I could have run for it. I made it to a giant stump and leapt up onto it to safety.

On the other side of the river, I could hear the raucous laughter of the Māori neighbours at my predicament as the ram circled the stump seeking its revenge. Unfortunately, the noise from across the river had carried way beyond me to the big house, and I could see someone at the window with binoculars directed straight at me in full view, standing up on the stump. Soon the prize ram was the least of my worries because a four-wheeled farm bike was on its way towards me from the manor.

When the bike arrived, a lean, horsy-looking woman leapt from the machine, and so did three mean-looking dogs. 'Who are you?' she demanded.

'Who are you?' I replied.

'I'm Ella,' she said, 'and, unlike you, I am on my own property!'

'Is that Salmonella?' I asked.

Perhaps it was unfair—even stupid—for me to call her 'Salmonella'. After all, she had never cooked poisoned food for me; she had never cooked for me at all. My experience with her was brief and almost entirely unrelated to food. It was just that because I was fishing for salmon and because her name was Ella, the two words blended into the one for me.

She stood silently for a while, looking up at me, still vulnerably positioned on the stump. She was not angry, or if she was, she certainly did not show it because her breeding was as evident as that of the sheep. In fact, she smiled at me, but it was piranha-like as if she was a flesh-eater rather than a vegetarian like the ram, and it certainly was not an enticing smile. She walked up to the now calm ram, straddling its back with both legs. It bleated as she released the lure from its ear, then after unravelling the line from its curled horn, she whacked its rump, sending it on its way.

'I've decided to let you go too,' she said coldly, unclipping the lure and rewinding the balance of the line. 'But you'll leave your fishing gear behind. And your fish. And you ought to consider yourself fortunate I didn't set the dogs on you. I certainly will next time!'

As I left, she unleashed a vicious whack across my rump with my surfcasting rod, and I learnt why the bay was called Whakakiwi. I could still hear the Māori fellas laughing as the ram escorted me to the first fence. But I walked proudly, knowing my fishing technique had been excellent and wishing I had been content with just three beautiful salmon.

SHY

HE WAS SLIM, fair-haired, with a neat crew cut and came from Israel. When he boarded, he said his name was Shy. I asked him if it was a nickname or short for something else, he said, 'No, just Shy.' He took no offence at my asking. I found out afterwards, that in Hebrew, his name meant gift and guessed his parents were pleased to have been gifted a child. The Australians on board hardly glanced at him, pausing only briefly in their raucous joking. A quiet Swiss couple smiled, and the tall Dane shook his hand as they introduced themselves.

When all the divers were on board, and as the sun dipped behind gum trees on the ridge, we cast off towards the Great Barrier Reef. As we passed out of the harbour, a dog barked, and a flock of birds, blue and red and screaming, flapped from a clump of trees.

'What was that?' asked a pasty-looking Englishman.

'Just galahs,' I said, 'Australian parrots, they make a lot of noise and shit on everything.'

Shy smiled a quick secretive smile that lasted only an instant. One of the Australians scowled, but the others ignored me as they opened another can of Fosters.

We ate our first meal on board. Some had a quiet drink or two afterwards; others read tour guides and diving manuals. Shy sat backed into a quiet corner, nursing a slow beer, carefully reading a thick blockbuster of a book. The Australians played drinking games and arm-wrestled.

'Hey Shylock,' one called, 'Wanna rassle me?'

I watched Shy's reaction.

He didn't smile, 'No thanks, couldn't match you guys.' He went to the bunkroom a little later. As he closed his book, I glimpsed the title, *War and Peace*.

Early the next day, the Divemaster briefed us before the first dive. Most of the group had just finished dive courses with him, part of the package on their Adventure Trip to the Antipodes.

'The sharks here—if you see any—will be beyond the drop-off and very deep, so don't worry about them. More of a problem is the bloody barracuda. Last year a diver lost some of his fingers feeding the fish. So keep your fingers and other extremities close to your body.'

He paused, laughing in advance at his own joke, and added, 'They go for the little bits because their jaws don't fit over a whole diver.' He continued, 'I'll be with the new divers; the rest of you are big enough and ugly enough to look after yourselves. So do your final check for your buddy, and then in we go.'

The viz was a hundred feet or more, the coral and fish life beautiful in the crystal clear water, a colossal cod cruised past covered in barnacles. The Divemaster led the way, surrounded by his wide-eyed entourage of novices, followed by the others, including Shy. I rode shotgun above and slightly behind the others with a handy overview. The Australians went a little deeper than the leading group, scattering some stingrays that were formation flying in slow motion.

A large school of trevally appeared over a ridge near the four Australians. The phalanx of agitated fish flashed gold and silver in the sunlight as they slanted first one way, then the other, heading directly towards us. Something was exciting them. From my vantage point, I could see why. Several barracuda were herding them, like dogs herding sheep. When the trevally approached our group, the loud-mouthed Australian waved both his arms wildly, and the trevally broke up into a dozen smaller groups and whirled away in all directions.

The nearest of the barracuda turned, paused, and went for the Australian trespassing on his patch, interfering with his hunt. It was far quicker than human reaction time, just a flash of dark turquoise light. It hit him in the upper arm tearing off a huge chunk of flesh in one vicious wrench. The novice divers horrified as a thick cloud of blood spread from the injury, turned panic-stricken upwards in an awkward random manner, some vainly clawing toward the surface. The Divemaster paused only briefly to make his decision, finning rapidly upwards to control and slow the ascent of the novice group he had earlier trained in the pool behind the dive shop.

The barracuda had moved off a little but were darting back and forth, still angry and agitated. The injured diver was struggling, his mask off, mouthpiece out, and blood billowing outwards from his arm. His mates had turned, rapidly and skillfully swimming upwards, joining the learner divers, finding comfort, like juvenile fish, in a bigger group. The regrouped school of humans, now firmly under the instructor's control, after he had slowed and calmed them, finned upwards toward the safety of the boat.

Only Shy, agile and swift, had decisively turned downwards, and I tentatively followed from far higher up. He seized the struggling diver, immediately replacing the mouthpiece hanging on the same side as the limp, bleeding arm and inflating his buoyancy vest a little. He rolled the diver over and began towing him slowly upwards. I met them on their long ascent and lent an additional towing arm, keeping a careful eye on the barracuda still sulking below.

On that slow ascent, I could feel the power of Shy's driving fins and the controlled thrust as his free arm reached upwards and palmed efficiently downwards. I saw him change his towing arm without missing a beat of his fins. I also noticed the identity chain around Shy's throat, designating his rank of captain in an elite Mossad assault group of the Israeli Army.

THE TACTICIAN

MICHELLE WAS ABOUT 28, had short dark hair, and when she smiled, she was charming, but mostly she had the forlorn look of someone trying to shake off a persistent sadness. She had never crewed on a yacht before joining the club and had only joined after she returned from Australia, doing so on the advice of friends who were trying to break her apparent malaise after her marriage broke up.

She was looking from one man to the other as each spoke, sensing an underlying animosity between them; it wasn't the words so much as the tone. Indeed, there was also a difference in their natures: Raymond Bentley, the Commodore of the Yacht Club, had a commanding presence, formally dressed in a reefer jacket, pressed slacks and an open-necked business shirt. The previous week he had invited Michelle to dinner after the prize giving. She surprised herself by accepting but had immediately wondered why she had done so. Perhaps she was flattered—maybe it would make her friends relax and get off her case when they found out she had begun socialising again.

The second man was quite different: self-effacing in his manner and casually dressed in jeans, sweatshirt and sneakers. Joe O'Donnell had invited her to crew with him, and she had accepted his invitation before she realised how important the final race of the season had become.

The new trophy, the Blake Memorial Shield, for the Best Overall Yachtsman, filled a gap in the club's trophy list and was hotly contested in its first year. Based on aggregate points, only two members could win the Blake trophy by the time of the last race. Raymond Bentley was marginally ahead of Joe O'Donnell. This last yacht race would determine the result; it was a two-person race in which one of each crew had to be a novice yachtsman.

Bentley, who had the faster boat, a sleek 45-footer, chose an experienced yachtsman as his crewman, but he was still defined as a 'novice' because he had never previously been a member of their particular yacht club. Some suspected that Bentley talked him into joining the club for that reason. Joe was the better sailor, but his boat was only 35 feet long, a Bruce Farr 1050. He had crewed for some of New Zealand's best yachtsmen and was regarded as a superb racing tactician.

'I'm glad you accepted the spot on Joe's boat,' Bentley said to her.

She sensed Bentley's surge of pleasure came from his self-interest, knowing that both his boat and his crew were superior, giving him a clear double advantage. Michelle thought there was something deeper between Joe and Ray and felt she was somehow being drawn unknowingly into their masculine competitive world.

Bentley reminded her of her other promise, 'I'm looking forward to taking you out for dinner after the prize-giving?'

'So am I,' Michelle replied. 'But I hope I don't first totally disgrace myself in the race.'

'More to the point,' said Bentley laughing, and sipping on his glass of wine, 'will be whether Joe gets you back in time for dinner.'

'Don't worry about the race Michelle, you'll be fine,' said Joe. 'And don't you worry, Ray—I like my meals on time too.'

Joe finished his Steinie, 'We'll see you both next week.' Bentley did not respond, just smiling as he watched Joe leave the clubrooms.

When Michelle went on board Joe's yacht, *Rendezvous,* she realised it was different from others she had boarded. It was a bit battered about in the galley area as if used regularly. There was a stained gas stove swinging on its hinges in the gentle swell. Plastic cups and plates were stacked in slots that protected them in a heavy sea. There were books on the slotted shelves, some on yachting and navigation, Grisham and Wilbur Smith novels, and older classics like *The Brothers Karamazov* by Dostoevsky. This yacht was not just a gin palace with girlie magazines and a cocktail cabinet.

Joe noticed her scrutiny and said, 'I have lived on board since I sailed back from the States about a year ago.'

'This is your home?' she asked in surprise. 'I feel a bit like an intruder.'

'Throw your stuff in the forward cabin,' he said. 'There's a loo there and a hand basin. Just make yourself at home. I use the aft cabin—it's nearer the wheel and the radio and everything else that matters when I'm at sea.'

They set out for the start line in a bit of a circuitous path as Joe demonstrated to her how they would sail Rendezvous and, in particular, the start and the first leg of the race. With his skill and the boat's nimble mobility, Joe and Michelle won the tactical start of the race, but Bentley quickly moved wide, catching an unexpected favourable wind shift and hit the front before the first buoy. He covered Joe, who tacked back and forth on the second leg doing everything possible to overhaul the bigger yacht with its greater area of sails. At the last buoy, as Bentley tried to set the spinnaker for the run home to the finish line, they got the big sail caught in the rigging. His boat speed dropped right off as he turned into the wind to untangle the sail. Joe pounced on Bentley's mistake. While setting the spinnaker, he waved at Michelle to bring the yacht hard around the buoy and gestured vigorously towards the finish. They slipped past the bigger boat at full speed, well before Bentley's spinnaker finally caught the wind and inflated. Joe fine-tuned their spinnaker and began stowing the mainsail while Michelle, at the helm with the wind whistling through her hair, forgot everything else as she focused on holding the shortest path to the finishing line. She knew they only had to cover the other boat; if Bentley tacked, either way, they could do the same, shutting out his wind, shutting out his chances. Well before his tacking skills were needed, she knew Joe would have finished stowing the mainsail.

Bentley was over 100 metres behind them in hot pursuit and slowly reducing the gap when Michelle felt the sand beneath the keel, and she was thrown against the wheel as the yacht ground to a halt. Bentley boat's line was offset marginally from Joe's and powered past on their starboard with Bentley waving jubilantly.

'I'm so sorry,' said Michelle to Joe. 'I never saw the sandbar.'

'I knew it was there and should have warned you,' Joe replied.

'But you were busy with the sails.'

'Never mind,' he said.

'What do we do now?' she asked.

'First thing, we might have a cup of coffee. The tide is on the ebb, and it'll be three hours to low, another three back to the present level. Maybe seven or eight hours before we can float off. Perhaps I should say sorry too?'

'Why?'

'You'll be late for dinner with Bentley.'

'Oh, Hell! I had forgotten all about that,' she said.

'He'll probably want to send the race patrol boat down for you.'

'But what about you?'

'There's an old tradition that the skipper stays on board the boat, even goes down with it!' He laughed pleasantly at their predicament.

'That doesn't seem fair, to leave you here, I put the boat on the bar, and I cost you the race—and the Blake trophy.'

'If Peter Blake were still alive, he would laugh at my predicament—wouldn't be the first time either.'

'You knew him?' she asked, incredulous.

'Oh, yes! I was on the big cat with him that went around the world.'

'Really! You're kidding me?'

Joe went to the bookshelf and pulled out an album. He flicked through to near the back and opened the album to a photograph at the reception in France.

'That's me with the champagne hairdo,' he laughed.

She sat down at the sloping table and looked at the photo of the crew celebrating their record circumnavigation of the globe. She went to turn back the pages, but Joe instinctively put his hand on hers to stop her.

'Don't! Please?' he said.

'Sorry, I didn't mean to pry.'

They fell silent; he removed his hand from hers. They were both embarrassed.

'What say you make the coffee while I finish stowing the sails.'

'That's a deal,' said Michelle, closing the album and handing it back to him.

He showed her how the gas stove worked, pointed out the coffee and the mugs, and told her the milk was in the fridge. While she made the coffee, she could hear him topside stowing the spinnaker.

The yacht leant over further as the tide ebbed lower, and they had to hold their hot coffee mugs clear of the sloping table.

'The boat should stop about where it is,' he said. 'We can still manage to walk around, and everything still works. Sorry about before, you can look at the rest of the photos if you like.'

'That's okay,' she said. 'Perhaps there are some pages in

our lives we shouldn't turn back. We all have the odd skeleton in the cupboard.'

The humming radio crackled to life: 'Well guys, we're back in the clubrooms, having a glass of bubbly, celebrating our win, thought a good tactician would know the sandbars and tides Joe. The last stragglers are just coming in, and then we'll send the patrol boat down to pick up Michelle. Winner takes all, eh Joe?'

Joe did not move. He just looked across the table at Michelle.

'Hullo, Joe? Hullo, Michelle? Is anyone home?' said Bentley.

Joe did not move.

'How does the radio work?' she asked.

'You just pick up the handpiece and press the little black button.'

Michelle made her way across the sloping carpet to the radio: 'Hullo Ray, this is the acting skipper of the Rendezvous —who feels duty-bound to stay on board until the tide floats us off. Over and out.' She put the handpiece back and turned the on-off switch. The humming of the radio stopped.

She took the bottle of bubbly she had seen on its side in the fridge, beside the two portions of fillet steak, and passed it to Joe, who smiled as he reached for glasses.

'Joe, I like your boat's name, *Rendezvous*,' she said. 'And now I know why they say you are a master tactician. And I'll help you with dinner later—if you want me to.'

THE OLD MAN AND THE SEA

THE OLD MAN'S favourite fishing spot was in the lee of Mayor Island, in a bay against a rock face, where only the remnant roots of a small tree he had once used as a marker remained. Over many years, he'd watched the small flowering tree grow, age, and die, and during each storm, a little more of the deadwood had fallen away. Subsequent weathering had left an exposed patch of volcanic basalt threaded with a seam of black argillite, hard and sharp, and that had become his new marker. He did well on that spot and, although the tree was gone, the sweet birdsong of the surrounding bush still sounded.

Sometimes, but only on calm days, he anchored a few kilometres away in the open sea above a little known reef. After creating a burley trail and waiting patiently for the fish to find the source and follow it up to be tempted by his baited hook, he usually secured a good catch. He smiled to himself when he saw younger men pulling up their anchors every half hour or so and crashing across the waves to another spot.

Today, though, was different. With his boat on the dry stand for repainting, he had agreed to make up the numbers for a fishing tournament on a marine equipment dealer's boat. In his late thirties, Harvey was a younger man, prominent on the club committee and in charge of the social function at the end of the three-day tournament.

The old man had nothing personal against Harvey but was conscious of rumours that had circulated a few years earlier: rumours about receiving free drinks from a barmaid later dismissed for theft; stories about free meals from the club caterer during lease negotiations. The questions were never adequately answered during Harvey's term as president because, he claimed, going into details would hinder good governance. The old man knew that good governance included transparency, accountability and the application of ethical principles, just as it required efficiency and well-directed performance. Harvey's explanation didn't fit with any of those criteria.

On the first day of the tournament, trolling in the deep water, they caught no fish, and the old man became tired, bouncing around in the slop and chop of the ocean.

Late in the day, he commented to the others, 'Even after splitting the expenses, this type of fishing seems costly and for little benefit.'

Two of the younger men laughed at him.

'The taxman subsidises my fishing!' stated one.

'Using a bit of cash from the fairies,' said another, smiling.

The old man raised his eyebrows at these comments. Both of them were employed by local businesses: one as a rep for a prominent manufacturer and the other as manager of a hardware shop.

Only Harvey, the boat dealer, with his hawk-like face and cold hard eyes, assessed the old man's words carefully and was more circumspect, 'Trolling for game fish is part of the club competition, it gives all of us, including you, a shot at the big prizes. For example, you might win a trip to Fiji.'

'I suppose I'm not used to chasing after big fish,' the old man replied casually.

He knew he didn't fit in. It's strange being here, he thought, I don't like these men, and obviously, they don't like me much either.

On the second day, the younger men caught four kingfish between them, none large enough to justify taking to the nightly weigh-in between the jetty and the clubrooms. The old man had caught nothing, trolling without enthusiasm in the open water. The three younger men didn't offer to give the extra fish to him with four fish among four men. He didn't complain, but he was angry when he overheard one whispering, 'The silly old goat couldn't catch a cold!' He left them on the stern deck, making himself a coffee on the gas cooker in the cabin.

The old man's distaste for them grew deeper each day, and the younger men sensed his judgment of them. There were unexplained innuendo and laughter in much of their conversation. Their foul language, comments about women, coarse stories, and almost everything about them grated with the old man. Their increased tempo of disgusting comments seemed designed to offend him, to convince him to exit the competition.

The old man kept to himself. His wife was gone now, his children all lived offshore, and these men, in a perverse way he couldn't fathom, stained memories of his wife and family, even of his own life and the way he'd lived it.

He resolved to stay home on the final day of the competition. But when he woke, he changed his mind. He'd complete the tournament with them, regardless of their behaviour. On the third day, to avoid the others and because he was naturally tidy, he made coffee for everyone, washed the cutlery and dishes from the previous day, and shoved the three days of accumulated rubbish into rubbish bags for taking ashore later. He wiped down the dusty surfaces and swept out the cabin, giving Harvey's boat something of an overdue spring clean.

His excess tidiness originated from years of employment in the accounts department of an importer. Order forms, delivery dockets, invoices, payment slips, receipts for every purchase, and every sale were reconciled manually in the early days and later by computer. Some of the younger ones called me a silly old goat then too, he thought, but the auditor always supported me, and eventually, I became manager. But the company was ripped off after I retired. They should've guessed it would happen: it was common knowledge the new manager was a sly drinker and had a fancy bird on the side, a smart-arse, just like this lot.

Out beyond the steaming volcano on White Island, as they turned for shore on the last day, the old fisherman found himself separate from the other men, jammed in the corner of the stern deck to counter the roll of the swell. His snow-white head nodded up and down to each rise and fall of the heavy sea. He was somewhere between sleep and consciousness, his mind dredging over old memories as the twin-diesels powered them back towards the shore.

His reverie was broken by a large swell that shuddered through the boat from bow to stern, compelling him to grip the rail. The younger men huddled in whispered conversation. The surge of water on the hull meant the old man picked up only fragments of what they planned for the prize-giving and the party that would follow. But he was now wide awake and had heard enough to arouse his suspicions.

Falling off to sleep again, he dreamed of earlier times when he started fishing: the snapper were bigger, and the activity of pulling in fat blue maomao from a school of hundreds, sometimes thousands, created a moving dark blue patchwork on the light blue sea. He remembered keeping a watch out for kingfish, attracted by the frenzy he was creating, and how he'd occasionally catch one of these large curious fish. Once, while reeling in a 20-kilo kingfish, a mako shark had scythed in close to the boat and taken the body of the kingie in one instinct-crazed snatch, leaving the old man with just the bloodied head. He woke with a start as he re-experienced the fear of the sloping teeth of the shark, gorging on the kingie so close to his small boat. Life's like that, he mused, small fish taken by predators. After I left, it happened with the company, but I did well enough out of the investigation when they needed me back to rework the figures. Without me, they'd never have proved a thing.

As they entered the mooring, Harvey, smiling, turned to him, 'How are you feeling, old man? Big day?'

'Sure thing. I normally sit in the island's lee and catch the odd snapper, or I get a few tarakihi out over the reef. That does me.'

'An early night then?'

'No, no,' said the old man. 'I might come along for a couple of beers.'

'Pity we didn't catch anything today; we would've shared it with you,' said the hardware manager.

'No problem,' replied the old man.

The old man went home, cleaned up, changed his clothes, and cooked a modest meal of fish fillets from his freezer. The party in the marquee was already at a full pitch when he pushed his way through the crowd. The fishermen had been well primed up during the day, drinking rum and beer on their boats, but that hadn't slowed down consumption. Women were popping bubbly and competing for the attention of the men with more and more abandon. They danced wildly, whirling past the old man, half-spilling his beer as they crashed into him. He merged back into the crowd, out of their way, nearer the bar.

The old man saw the problem arising before anyone else: first, the Lion Red ran out and then, as the drinkers focussed on the less popular lines, it was clear they would run out as well. Then, as brands became scarce, the grumbling became severe.

'Who ordered the grog?' demanded a young, unshaven fisherman, looking for a Speight's Dark and cursing when offered a light lager, 'Na! It's weasel piss and goes straight through ya!' His mates laughed.

The old man didn't laugh; he'd disappeared outside and was somewhere down in the car park.

Harvey stood on a crate and tried to silence the grumbling men. He weathered their insults and waited for silence. 'We allowed $40 a head for drink, and you've cut it out in record time,' he said, laughing. The men booed and jeered, and the women shouted abuse at him. He held his hands up again for silence, and when the crowd noise lulled, he said, 'We can get more drink if that's what you want.' The crowd cheered. 'But we'll have to send a bucket around for cash to help pay for it.' The cheering stopped, replaced by a sullen silence.

Brand new plastic buckets appeared from nowhere, each with a local hardware sticker on its side, and a well-known company rep chucked a $50 note in the nearest bucket. Harvey followed suit with several $20 notes; those around him cheered and reached in their own pockets for money. Finally, the mumble of discontent changed to a muted celebration as they all helped solve the problem.

'We've drunk the place dry!' claimed one patron with pride. The buckets began their rounds. Harvey thanked them for their generosity, stepped down off the crate, and wandered back to his group of friends.

The old man returned. He pushed forward, stepped up on the same crate, and shouted, 'Are you all stupid?' An angry buzz went through the crowd. Then, someone who knew the old man from way back shouted, 'Shut up and listen!'

The flow of money into the buckets stopped, and the drinkers went quiet.

'This is a ripoff! At five dollars a beer, forty bucks would get you eight beers each. Right? I'll bet there's not a man here who's had eight beers since the bar opened. And if you've had eight drinks today, half of them would have been your own beer on your own boats.'

The old man stopped, surprised at his steady voice, clear

and resonant but as hard and sharp as the argillite seam on Mayor.

Harvey pushed forward and dragged the old man off the crate.

'What the hell do you think you're playing at?' he hissed at the old man. 'Shut your mouth, or I'll shut it for you.'

But it was too late: while many of the club members were nearly drunk, they were not yet stupidly so. Some compared notes on how many drinks they had consumed; one counted on his fingers; some just grumbled. The women who had been loudest in celebration became loudest in objection.

'Three glasses of cheap bubbly is not worth forty bloody bucks either!' shrieked one.

The old man was pushed forward by those around him and hoisted back on the crate. 'There's more drink alright, under a tarp on the hardware truck—about a hundred dozen, by my estimate. And if you add that to what you've already drunk, it would total about what you paid as an entry fee. So, it's your booze out there—and it's yours without paying another cent. On the other hand…' He paused, quite deliberately, knowing they would wait for him to finish. 'On the other hand—if 200 of you put $20 each in the bucket—that's $4,000 in the pockets of those behind this scam.' He stepped down and left the marquee as pandemonium broke out.

Despite not catching a single fish in the tournament, the old man went home and slept easy, hearing the gentle rumble of the sea in his dreams.

UNDERWATER GARDEN

GETTING to a particular dive site on Great Barrier Island was not easy. It took most of a day on the ferry from central Auckland, with my Holden ute on board, suffering the rolling swell for the four-hour trip. I had thrown an old mountain bike on the back of the ute, along with my freediving gear, including a one-piece wet suit, fins, goggles, gloves, catch bag and other necessary items. I had booked a BnB near Tryphena Harbour, where the ferries make regular trips to and from Auckland. So my five-day week on Barrier meant only three days diving. I intended to dive around the outward-facing east coast, venturing out to a different remote bay each day before returning to my BnB to rest and eat at one of the modest cafés.

The BnB owner saw my gear on my ute and said, 'You look as if you have come over for some serious cold-blooded killing!'

'That's not what I do,' I replied. 'I am careful to select what I kill to help sustain marine life for the future. For instance, I avoid killing alpha males who father the vast majority of fish and crayfish.' He seemed sceptical and said, 'So you place a greater value on the life of the strong than the weak?' I was not unduly concerned by his comments, which seemed a little argumentative to me.

On my first day, I drove the ute up a poorly maintained road over a range, and then, for a brief time, I thought to bike down the other side but soon decided the track was far too rough. I would need to climb down carrying my gear.

I carefully made my way down through the renewing forest cover of manuka, kanuka and older pohutukawa, their roots embedded deep into the rocky gully and embraced by an ecosystem of lilies, ferns and climbing rata. The thick horizontal branches were hosts to lichen and moss, and other dependents. I glimpsed a view of a kauri ricker that had 20 more years as a simple fir tree before it could cloudburst to become a local Tane Mahuta. I heard but did not see a sweet chiming kokako.

My stumbling journey created an unwelcome bubble of

silence. The dawn chorus of birdlife was prolific, but it silenced as I traversed my path down, only to recommence above me as I descended a little further. I knew my 20-minute descent would be an hour-long return.

I ate one of my filled rolls and sipped from my Powerade as I rested on what passed for a beach, patches of bare rock with the odd spinifex seeking a fertile anchoring spot. I could see gannets diving on a kilometre-wide school of fish further out, closer to Arid Island. I thought they were probably plundering baitfish above a school of kawhai, and in all likelihood, kingfish were cruising lower down.

Closer to the shoreline, there were many protruding boulders making access from fishing boats quite hazardous. The situation seemed perfect.

I geared up and clambered down the last rocky face and, after a short swim, found myself in a beautiful underwater garden. It had a series of narrow vertical cracks containing dozens of crayfish behind stalked kelp and hanging seaweed bright and variegated from the sun's rays. The rocks were a mixture of browns, reds and other pastel colours from past volcanic activity. Some of the boulders had a bluish-green tinge reflecting the presence of seams of copper. Upon my approach, the crayfish retreated deeper into their recessed hiding places.

I noticed an octopus suddenly appear deeper down. It was slithering from crack to crack, following my path. The octopus seemed to watch me closely as I reached deep into a crevice, seized the horns of a cray, and wrenched it out. The cray was wildly flapping its tail, so I turned it upside down, and it settled down. Jokingly, I offered it to the staring octopus. A couple of tentacles reached upward tentatively, which surprised me. Every octopus I had ever encountered had been timid, avoiding direct contact.

The octopus thought better of its approach and withdrew its tentacles and drew itself back a little. The octopus was male and larger than any other I had seen, although clearly of the same common species. Perhaps, he had prospered here, and perhaps, his size allowed him to chase off competitors. I found his actions intriguing but did not imagine what was to ensue.

I swam to the surface, about ten metres above, put the crayfish in my catch bag hanging from my float and carried on with my swim, forgetting the octopus for a time.

Further around the little bay, I found a colony of paua. I removed a scraper from my catch bag and flicked some of the paua free, placing them in the bag.

Later, after carefully approaching a shallow area where waves were breaking on the shoreline, I speared two modest fish, a snapper and trevally. On my return swim back to my entry point, I secured a second crayfish. The same octopus was in the same underwater garden, seemingly awaiting my return, and approached closer, changing marginally in colour from green to a reddish hue, seeming to signal his presence deliberately. Clearly, he had remembered my earlier offer and was perhaps hoping I would do so again. I did not oblige but was amazed by this second direct approach, indicated once more by a noticeable colour change.

Back at the BnB, the owner was impressed with my catch but asked me, 'How can you possibly eat all of that?'

'Come over to the café later, and you'll see,' I replied, not explaining that I had spoken with the café manager the previous evening.

I enjoyed half a crayfish with salad and chips and a couple of beers free of charge, leaving the café manager able to offer the other three halves to his customers at a special price. He also agreed to use the paua and fish to make a seafood chowder the following evening, claiming it would make at least a dozen bowls as well as one for us both. I suggested that a few trimmings from the cray halves would enhance the mix, and he nodded his assent. Later, he put the cooked cray legs and claws in a couple of baskets and placed them on the bar counter as a free snack for his regulars.

I slept fitfully that night; early evening and early morning owls were calling each other. I dreamed they were in a shed in the scrub behind my bedroom, and the BnB owner had installed them to pay me back for his perceived excesses of my harvesting of seafood.

In the morning, I realised there was no shed in the bush. The owner was working with his compost bins, emptying the third bin through a sieve and bagging the dry mix. Then he shovelled the second bin, covered with a polythene sheet, into the final bin alternating the compost with layers of sheep pellets. Because of the sheet, it was teeming with worms. Then he did the same with the first bin, mixing in grass clippings and ashes. He had a large pile of material ready to put in the first bin.

'Pretty impressive,' I said.

'Works okay,' he replied, 'The worms seem to enjoy it, and so do my vegetables.' I wondered if he was making a point, but there was no edge in his voice.

Despite my earlier intention to dive at a different location each day, I returned to the same underwater garden the second morning. I had always found octopi to be lovely, intelligent creatures, timid and non-confrontational. This octopus seemed unique, as if it had been communicating with me the previous day, and I was curious to observe it some more.

However, there was no sign of the octopus until I was well beyond the garden and reached the deeper ocean floor, where it magically reappeared among a cluster of boulders by resuming the same reddish-brown colour of the previous day. When I held a new cray out, the octopus reached out with its tentacles and did not touch the crayfish, but one slender tentacle wrapped around my free wrist, and I felt the suckers on my bare arm and touching the luminous dial of my wristwatch. Three more tentacles reached out, touching my fins, wetsuit and dive mask, but in an exploratory way, rather than with any aggression. I calmly wrapped my gloved fingers lightly around one tentacle, but this was a step too far for the beast, and it withdrew its tentacles beyond my reach. But it did not retreat as it had the first day. This time it remained close and slowly reapproached me. Perhaps it was testing my goodwill or even my resolve; I was confused by its behaviour.

I knew that octopi hunted mostly at night, waiting for its prey to come out in the dark before ambushing them. They could not extract crayfish as I did because they could not grasp them, and the crayfish could jam themselves tightly in the back of their recess.

The tentacles seemed to focus now on the crayfish, and once it had a firm grip, it drew itself closer in a strange forward rolling motion, as if on four tentacle wheels, and he ballooned out like a parachute, rapidly engulfing the cray and my hand. I felt the suckers selectively releasing my gloved hand, but not the crayfish, which was struggling to escape.

The octopus enveloped its prey, and its hard beak crunched through the shell and pumped in a paralysing fluid. Then, in one frantic motion, it sucked the nutrients from the carcass of the crayfish. Although it only took a few seconds, the slitted eyes watched me during this process, assessing my response. My staring eyes remained as neutral as those of my accomplice in this act of predation. Only then did I notice that two tentacles had earlier reached around my waist, preventing me from retreating during his attack.

In that instant of time, my view of the octopus world changed forever. This octopus was a cunning attacker and, seemingly, had no intention of allowing me to stand in his way. He invited my involvement by signalling his presence, a direct reversal of colour changes to hide. Instead, he had used this unique ability to attract my attention.

I took a small crayfish and a modest snapper back and gave them to the BnB owner, who was pleasantly thankful and said he would get a carton of vegetables for me before my departure.

On the third day, the octopus waited secretively for me in an even deeper area well past the garden, drawing attention to himself with a similar colour change. I now believe he did this entirely in self-interest. He approached me to take the crayfish as soon as I had wrenched one free. He devoured it in the same violent manner as before, again linking some tentacles around my waist or legs, enforcing my complicity.

After the octopus had gorged himself, he led me deeper down by alternating his colour pattern, and I followed him through a disguised crack that took us beyond the bay where we had been swimming each day, out into the open ocean. The snapper were much larger on the outer face, and I shot a fish weighing about 10 kg. I felt a little guilty because it was a large breeding male, and I had broken one of my cardinal rules. I would give the whole fish to the café manager for whatever use he wished.

The octopus watched me fix the fish on the spike attached to my float. I wondered if he was deliberately rewarding me for the crayfish I had just procured. I did, however, suspect he had followed me the previous day when I had speared the two smaller fish and had guessed my intention in the open ocean.

He went deeper again, about 15 metres, his colours going red-green, red-green, several times. I took a deep breath and plunged downward in answer to his call. Beyond the octopus was a horizontal overhang with a recessed shelf. I peered into the gloom, seeing a colony of giant packhorse crayfish, the larger species of rock lobster.

When they saw me, they did not immediately back into their recess but braced themselves for a hasty retreat, standing their ground in the meantime. Some of the packhorses would have weighed 15 kilograms or more. I was gobsmacked; the octopus was openly trading with me: small fish for small lobster; big fish for giant lobster! I left the packhorses and swam back to the surface.

On other dives, I had seen the accumulation of shells, crab carcases, and small crayfish remains around the entrances of octopus dens, the signs of the occupants eking out a modest living, signs of the balance that I thought nature seeks to achieve.

When I surfaced, I noticed the sky had clouded over, and the wave action had marginally increased. We returned to the inner bay and swam together towards the shore, the octopus pulsating through the water below, alternately sucking in water then squirting it out behind me, without any colour changes. The overcast conditions meant there was no sunlight in the underwater garden. He may have already guessed our hunting partnership had ended; I had learned that beneath the surface of the ocean, nature had its own rules in which I was usually only an observer.

But I was uncomfortable participating in a strange Darwinian adaptation, helping change a usually friendly species into a mass killer.

MOVE OVER KID

HE WAS ONLY 12 years old, but he was a pretty good fisherman; he had learned his skills from his grandfather, I believe. His father was a high-end lawyer and didn't know his bait from his backside. His mother, who travelled around the country demonstrating microwave cooking, hated going on boats and would throw up at the sight of a goldfish bowl, so he certainly never learned much about fishing from his parents.

During the May school holidays, both of his parents were travelling away on business, so they booked him on our annual three-day fishing charter until they were due back. The skipper told us he wanted to use the opportunity to get a credit against a conveyancing bill with the father's law firm, and we said that would be fine with us. No one said anything, but some thought the lad would puke as soon as we hit the open sea swell and then spend most of the three days on his bunk.

The first ominous sign was when he took a carborundum block out of his tackle box and started rubbing a concave point on the hook of his sparkling greenstone lure. He kept holding the hook up to the light and checking it until he thought it perfect and then deftly fixed it to his trace with a 98% knot. He sprayed a little CRC into his reel mechanism, and before we were outside the entrance, he was waiting on the port side of the stern with his rod ready. We found this a bit disconcerting because we were casual fishermen on our annual break from the drudgeries of life. So my mates rushed around to get their rods out, more out of pride than any need, and they were soon busy untangling old birds' nests and cutting away rusty hooks. Steve had been on the grog the night before, and the two-metre swells and his smelly old bait box were enough to get him heaving up over the back handrail.

The lad ignored Steve's noisy digression and had his first strike before any of us were anywhere near ready. The skipper throttled back, and the young fellow reeled the kahawai in like a pro, and we gaffed it and hauled it on board for him. He immediately bled the fish and threw it in the icebox.

By the time the skipper had the boat back up to speed, he had his line back in the water, still over in the port corner, and the three of us were at last ready to fish. As we lined up to put our lines out, he caught his second kahawai. He reeled it in, bled it, and chucked it with the first one in the icebox. Before the boy had the chance to put his line back in the water, Mike had made his bid for the boy's space.

'Move over, kid!' said Mike. 'Looks like you got the lucky side, and we are paying customers.'

The lad just shrugged, shifted sides, and before long had a strike from the starboard corner and reeled in his third kahawai. The same thing again—he bled it and chucked it straight in the icebox.

'They're striking from the outsides inwards,' said Mike. 'You take the other side, Steve.'

'Move over, kid,' said Steve.

So the lad ended up next to me in the middle of the stern.

Mike had a strike, but he lost the fish and cursed when he tried to set the hook, claiming, 'That was a big sod, would've been the best so far—easy!'

By now, Steve and Mike were getting angry, and about eleven o'clock got their first cans of beer out of the icebox. At about one o'clock, we arrived at our lunch spot in the lee of Motiti Island, and the skipper dropped the anchor.

'Pity we haven't got a smoker; we could have smoked a kahawai,' said the skipper.

'I can cook it another way,' offered the boy.

'Go for it!' I said. 'If you cook anything like you catch fish, I'll try it.'

'Help yourself to whatever you need,' said the skipper.

'Kahawai is bloody junk unless it's smoked,' said Mike.

'Even then, they're all skin and bone. Leave me out too,' added Steve sullenly. 'I might just have another can.'

Using a razor-sharp knife, the lad conventionally filleted two of the fish, skinned the fillets, carefully cut away the seams of red meat, and then cut the flesh into rectangles about the size of thick hash browns. He got the gas going in the galley, and while the big fry pan was heating up, he sliced a lemon into about ten thin pieces. He wrapped each piece of fish up in a flat piece of foil with a thin slice of lemon on the top of the flesh. He placed them all in the hot pan and pressed them hard down to make close contact between the foil-wrapped fish and the heavy metal base. While they sizzled, he spread some bread with margarine and stacked it on a dinner plate. He looked at his watch and flipped each foil package over. While he waited, he packed the fish carcasses in a plastic bag for the cray pots and threw them back in the icebox. No doubt watching his mother demonstrate food preparation and cooking for her occasional guest appearance on television had taught him a thing or two.

The skipper and I were watching with increasing interest and sat down at the cabin table. Steve and Mike opened another can, each on the stern deck trying to ignore the aroma of the sizzling fresh fish drifting their way from the galley.

The boy put the pan on a thick mat in the middle of the table beside the plate of bread and said, 'The idea is to unwrap the foil and make a fish sandwich between two thick bits of fresh bread, like this.' He demonstrated, sinking his teeth into the first sandwich, adding, 'One advantage of this method is that there is no washing up to do. I call them fish butties.'

Steve came into the cabin, followed closely by Mike, and

said, 'That smells so good! Mike and I can't wait any longer for lunch.' He laughed a little sheepishly, adding, 'Move over, kid!'

WILLY

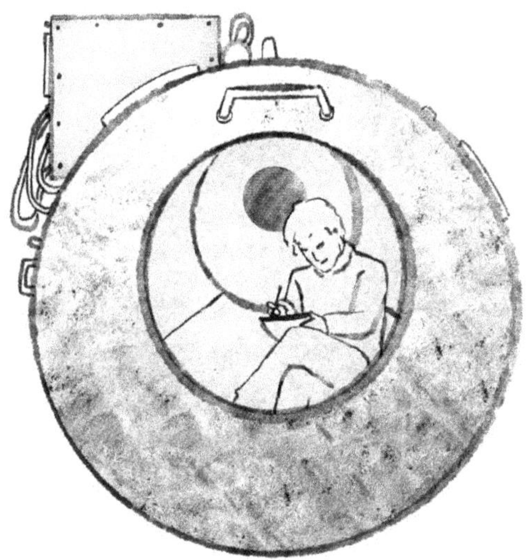

DEAR UNCLE HARRY

I thought you would be interested to know how my first dive went. The Mount Underwater Club had a trip going to Plate Island, so along I went. They seemed a friendly lot and even arranged a diver called Fred to 'buddy' with me. He was big and fit, very tanned, and had done hundreds of dives. He helped me gear up in your old BC, your weight belt, catch bag, and so on. He told me attaching a knife and catch bag to the weight belt wasn't always a good idea. He seemed a little nervous about me—I don't know why—and kept on saying things like, 'You stick real close to me … all the time … understand?'

Fred said we would go down the anchor chain. The skipper told us it was about 30 metres at the anchor and a lot deeper under the boat at the dive site. Anyway, he jumped in, and I waddled across the deck with all your gear on, which wasn't comfortable with the boat rolling about. Not like the pool where I did my dive course.

So I put my mouthpiece in, held my mask just like I had been taught, and jumped in, just about landing on the top of Fred. As soon as I hit the water, I realised you use a lot more weights than me because I started sinking really fast. But luckily, I was right in front of Fred, and so, as I was dropping past him, I grabbed both of his legs, one under each arm. He had said to stick real close to him, and here I was taking his advice straight away.

I was going to inflate your BC, but Fred was struggling and, I had to hold on with both hands and couldn't reach the button. When I looked up, Fred was flailing around trying to get his mouthpiece into his mouth.By now, the surface was about five metres up and receding quite quickly. Thankfully, Fred had stopped struggling because he was busy clearing his mask, and then he had to clear his ears. Fortunately, I didn't need to clear anything, and I just hung on as we plunged into the deep blue yonder, scattering lots of pretty fish in our path.

It seemed more like a tandem parachute jump than a dive, and as I saw the floor of the sea rapidly approaching, I began to worry about a crash landing on the boulders directly below us. After all, we didn't actually have a parachute on. But then

I could hear the sound of rushing air as Fred inflated his BC at full throttle, and I felt our descent pulling up, just like with a parachute. And so we settled down, Fred's BC fully inflated, and mine dead flat. We were sitting facing each other on top of a giant round boulder with Fred's legs, and fins still shoved one under each of my arms. His eyes were bulging almost out of their sockets, and he didn't look at all tanned. In fact, he was pretty pale. Funny how some people are affected by depth.

Fred grabbed his complicated-looking computerised gauge system, which sounded like a pager beeping away, and pointed at it frantically. It showed 50, which relieved me considerably, and I couldn't work out why Fred was wildly gesticulating upwards. So I looked at my gauge, and it was on 165 feet, and I realised his gauge was metric, and the beeping was his computer alarm.

Fred reached forward and held down the button on my BC, and I felt the surge of air, giving us positive buoyancy. He grabbed me under both my upper arms and kicked off from the top of the boulder, and we started floating upwards, holding each other like dancing partners. As we ascended, his eyes became less bulged, his tanned skin returned, and he developed a grim smile on his face.

About halfway up, I realised my BC was still slowly making air, and I remembered you told me the button sometimes sticks down. Fred's alarm started beeping, his smile disappeared, and his eyes bulged again as we accelerated upwards. He held onto me with just one hand and discharged his BC with the other, and we slowed a little —only briefly. My BC was getting tighter and tighter and tighter as the leaking air trickled in, and again we accelerated upwards. In desperation, he violently wrenched on the tube where it joins the BC, and air gushed out. Once again, our ascent matched the speed of our bubbles and Fred's alarm stopped beeping, and we ascended slowly to the surface, both of us now about the proper buoyancy. We surfaced reasonably close to the boat, and Fred followed me as I paddled towards the ladder.

Unfortunately, my BC was discharging air faster than it was leaking in past the sticky button, and I started sinking again. My lunge for the ladder missed, and so did Fred's lunge for me. I was a little bit frightened because Fred had wrecked your BC. The bottom rushed up quicker this time because Fred's BC was not there to slow me down. And I could not inflate yours. It was then that I remembered the club Captain's pep talk on the boat before we left, 'If you get into trouble, remember to drop your weight belt, just drop it!' So I flicked the buckle open, and while it crashed to the floor of the sea, I bottomed out nicely in a stand-up position, gently stirring up a cloud of silt—just like the men landing on the moon.

Even without your weight belt, catch bag, cray hook and knife, I was still a bit heavy on down there and had to kick off and swim pretty hard to get an ascent going, and gradually it became more relaxed, and about halfway up, I was floating upwards with no effort at all. The last 20 metres or so was a lot trickier as I started to accelerate out of control. I stuck my fins out to the side like duck's feet to create some extra drag, and rhythmically flapped my palms upwards, a sort of downwards flying action, the reverse of a flying duck. I think it helped a bit, but I still rocketed up out of the water, like a Polaris missile being launched from a submarine. Fortunately, I was so close to the ladder that I grabbed the third rung up and climbed onto the deck as easy as pie.

On the boat, it was pure bedlam: the Club Captain was winding on the handle of a siren thing that was going 'ooga,

ooga, ooga', like a submarine about to submerge; someone else had the oxygen bottle out and was rigging it up; divers were returning to the boat so fast, it was as if sharks were chasing them.

'What's up?' I asked Fred.

'Keep away from me!' he said, cringing backwards.

I don't know why he was so upset; after all, it was me who had tingling joints.

And here I am in the Navy recompression chamber in Auckland because he wrecked your BC. Sorry about your gear Uncle Harry, but it was getting pretty old anyway, and it doesn't pay to hook your knife and catch bag to your weight belt like that. The club is going to Mayor Island later in the year, and if I can get some more gear, I want to dive out there. But I don't think I'll dive with Fred again, and I prefer someone who doesn't crack under pressure.

KAFKA'S KAFE

THEY WERE AN ODD COUPLE: Suzy was tiny, slim, and only a little over a metre and a half tall, while Jack was muscular with a two-metre frame. People often laughed, seeing them walking hand in hand; even on the train between Vienna and Prague, they had attracted a few second glances.

'Prague will be better than Vienna,' stated Jack, his 100 kilos supporting his brash confidence.

'I loved Vienna,' Suzy replied, 'the prancing Spanish Horses, the exquisite recital by the Vienna Youth Orchestra, the lovely palaces.'

'Too touristy for me,' said Jack. 'Give me a vibrant city any time: Barcelona rather than Madrid; Sydney rather than Melbourne. Prague will be more interesting than Vienna. Just wait and see.'

Their banter on the train never ceased. They argued about who would face forward in their seats and who would face backward. They argued about who would have the white checkers and who would use the black checkers on the board games they played. Jack would get physical to enforce his choice, and Suzy would usually trick him with her quick-wittedness.

The train was passing through open farmland when Suzy nervously raised the one contentious matter between them.

'Jack, you said we would discuss our future on this trip. I thought we had agreed we'd get married soon after we return from Europe.'

Jack was careful and deliberate in his answer: 'We get on so well—just as we are—why would we want to risk spoiling it all—by getting married?'

'Well, this will be the third time you have broken your word like this. And that's no answer anyway. You're a scuba instructor and want to start your own dive shop, and I want to have children. I could keep my job as the office manager in the law firm and help you with all the office work while you focus on running the gym. Once your own business is up and running, I could give up my job and handle the shop reception. And even bring our first little dive trainee along to work.'

Jack hesitated, struggling for an answer, 'But why right now?'

'After your wonderful results in this year's open water swimming events, you're now at your most popular. It would help if you started up while you're coaching so many tri-athletes, dive students, and pool swimmers. You should take the plunge now—while you're hot!'

Jack fell silent.

'And I'm thirty in a month, and from now on, our chances of having children will steadily drop off,' added Suzy.

'I know you're right,' Jack paused. 'I'm just waiting for some defining moment.'

'Well, that mystifies and disappoints me. Frankly, I don't even know what you mean. What are you waiting for: patterns in a teacup, a message in the sky?'

Suzy shifted away from Jack and looked out the window to hide her tears.

'We'll both know when it happens.' Jack was nervously clenching and unclenching his fist.

'I think it is fear that makes you delay—fear of the unknown; fear of not measuring up in business; but mostly, fear of yourself.'

'I've been accused of all sorts of things in my life, but never fear!'

Suzy turned away and took out her Czech phrasebook while Jack watched the changing countryside.

He was uncomfortable with the dissent and wanted to re-ignite their earlier friendly banter. He pointed through the train window at a group of large chalets: 'Look at those lovely houses on the riverbank. Real people live there, real people living real lives in real houses. Not like Vienna. I think Prague will be great!'

Suzy looked up, frowning, severe and silent, as the train emerged from the curved river gorge and a small town jiggled into view. Apartment buildings, long and grey, stretched back behind the smoking chimneys of huge industrial buildings. The street, covered with a mixture of snow and mud, was churned into ridges of grey slush. The buildings had the blandness of the central planners of the earlier Soviet era. A group of children pushed and shoved a small boy who had dropped his schoolbag and fell crying in the brown slush.

'Idyllic, isn't it—just like our lives?'

The village passed out of sight, and the train entered the outskirts of Prague. Suzy carried on reading the Czech phrasebook, repeatedly trying to pronounce words of greeting and expressions of please and thank you.

'It's difficult,' she said. 'They don't have many vowels in their words. How can you possibly pronounce that?' She pointed at a word, and Jack studied it.

'Fizz-spit-lick,' he replied.

'And what about that?'

Jack paused: 'Lick-spit-fizz. The same: only back to front.'

'Well, I prefer German. At least, it looks more like English.'

'We'll manage. We always do,' Jack said.

'Only because I do all the talking,' she replied.

'You smile; strangers see how beautiful you are. I know when to keep quiet. You say a few simple words of their language, like *bonjour* or *gracias*. Even if they have no idea what you are talking about, they help us. We're a good partnership, and that's the only reason I travel with you.'

'Thanks, Jack! That word doesn't even look like Fizz-spit-lick.'

'They all look like Fizz-spit-lick!' he replied. 'Like a secret code, or words in that game where you get slowly hung each time you can't get a letter. I always hated that game.'

Suzy looked up from her book: 'I was good at *Hangman* at school. Always got the word out or hanged the other person.' She paused.

'Did you know the Czechs invented the game of Hangman?' she asked slyly. 'Some of the best Hangman words like lynch and yacht were derived from the Czech language. Some words are from the spooky stories of Kafka, who lived in Prague. He wrote about the soulless government, about the murder of careless tourists in dark alleyways, or the torture of children in the crypts of old churches.'

Jack looked across at Suzy, who kept a straight face for as long as she could. When at last she smiled he realised she was tricking him. He grabbed her knee again to punish her, but eventually, it turned into a bear hug. Jack was pleased to have eased the tension between them, but he knew Suzy was far from happy.

The train skirted the city and stopped at the regional station just north of Prague. Suzy purchased a three-day transport pass for them both and found the Metro line to the city. As they picked up their bags and waited, an old lady trudged by pushing a heavy ablution cart with mops and brooms pointing skyward and clanking metal buckets hanging from it. Her eyes were vacant, lifeless, her lined grey face and worn-out body showing the ravages of decades of hard work in a harsh regime.

'Democracy has arrived too late for the old and poor of the Czech Republic,' said Suzy.

'People our age are happier, though,' Jack replied.

Suzy had worked out that when they arrived in the labyrinth of tunnels beneath Wenceslas Square, they could get to the tram-stop for their accommodation by crossing a diagonal tunnel beneath the square. But Jack, carrying the two big bags, called, 'Follow me', as he charged up the stairs of the closest exit. So they emerged onto the swarming square in the peak hour of early evening.

Jack sat their bags on the ground between them while Suzy studied her map again. Almost immediately, a group of local thieves approached them. Jack was preoccupied, gazing at the dark-silhouetted statues at the far end of the ancient square and the huge, flashing coloured signs of Coca Cola and Sony on the facades of historic medieval buildings. The local youths edged closer.

'We have company,' said Suzy quietly. 'Behind you, at least three of them.'

Jack turned, stepped forward and beckoned to the closest youth. As the man backed away, Jack smacked one big fist into his open palm in imitation of what he would do if he tried to touch them or their bags. As the group disappeared into the crowd to search out a softer target, Jack shouted, 'Fizz-spit-lick!' after them.

'We can go anywhere, do anything,' claimed Jack laughing. 'Your brains, my body.'

'We catch the tram over there,' said Suzy, but she was not smiling. They crossed the square and the adjoining street to the tram stop. A double-jointed electric tram whined up, and they crammed into a corner with their bags and headed for their *pensione*, according to Suzy, seven stops out that line.

The next day, they visited the Royal Palace and its surrounding markets. Next, they saw the Romanesque Saint George Church, an ancient structure built for simple

Christians of a millennium past—all contained within the Prague Castle precinct. Inside Saint Vitus Cathedral, the stonework was intricate, austere and reeking of a dark history. Finally, they crossed the River Vltava back to the city on the statue-lined Charles Bridge, passing buskers, hawkers and others, all trying to extract hard currency from tourists.

They lunched at a brightly lit little café where Jack ordered two fizz-split-licks by pointing at them in the food display. The young lady thanked him politely in English while smiling knowingly at Suzy, who whispered, 'Grow up!' to Jack

Later, as the afternoon darkened, they peered through the fence into the macabre Jewish Cemetery where Kafka and his parents had been buried, along with 10,000 others interred in multiple layers. The headstones formed a chaotic jumble of agonised faces, gargoyles, angels with broken wings, and other examples of macabre imagination. Most had a covering of dark green and brown lichens, mosses and weeds; Suzy said, 'Gosh, it's so spooky!' Jack laughed.

Jack and Suzy entered a maze of narrow medieval alleyways in the quickening twilight, intending to work back towards the better-lit restaurant area. However, among the closeness of the twists and turns, Suzy lost all sense of direction and became concerned as anonymous figures retreated into the shadows of recessed doorways leading to decrepit shops and dismal apartments.

Ahead of them, a flickering light with the words KAFKA'S KAFE glowed from a back-street bar, and as they reached the dim but welcoming entrance, a young couple turned into the alley in front of them. They were laughing and joking in their own language and heading for the bar.

'Let's ask them for directions,' said Suzy. 'We should get out of here.'

The couple soon recognised Suzy and Jack as tourists and spoke in German, French, and Spanish, trying to establish their nationality.

'Ah Engleesh!' the man guessed at last. 'Come weeth us. We are celebrating.'

They grabbed Jack and Suzy by their arms and pulled them towards the bar. Suzy resisted, but Jack said, 'They're okay. We'll have one drink here, get proper directions, and then find our way out.' Suzy reluctantly acceded.

The bar, dimly lit, with a series of partitioned cubicles, held small groups of people. Privacy seemed important because, as they entered, some patrons retreated into their booths until they realised it was just a group of laughing young people. The barman waved them through to the rear, where there was an empty booth against a lime-washed brick wall.

The man translated, and Jack ordered a glass of local wine for Suzy and a pilsener for himself because Suzy had told him Czech brewers were famed for that style of beer. In the dim light, they looked at their newly found friends. The woman shed her expensive, knee-length suede jacket. Suzy noticed that she wore a beautiful pendant around her throat and had glittering rings on both hands. Jack and Suzy sipped their drinks, enjoying the company of this happy pair until a tall man appeared before them. At first, Jack thought the man in the dark coat was the barman returning, but Suzy had seen the grim-faced man emerge from the darkness of another booth. He hauled a heavy handgun from his pocket and shouted, 'Na shledano Viliam!' He shot the man in the chest. Blood splattered in all directions.

The woman screamed, '*Ne! Gregor, ne!*' and he shot her too, twice. This time blood spurted across the table onto Jack, who froze in fear, and he could neither move nor speak.

The victims were silent and motionless. He swung the gun towards Suzy, a puzzled look on his face.

'*Dobre vecer Gregor. Mluvite Anglicky?*' asked Suzy.

The man with the gun, grim and sarcastic, replied, 'Good evening to you too. Yes, I speak English and four other languages. Who are you?'

'We're tourists and entered this bar at the same time as …'

'My wife … Gretchen … and her cheating lover.'

'I wondered …' said Suzy, her voice quivering.

'Wondered what?' Gregor demanded.

'Your wife is … was wearing beautiful rings.'

'*Ja* … yes, we were married, Gretchen and I … but that meant little to her.'

He flung her suede jacket aside and slid into the semi-circular booth next to his dead wife; he was now opposite Suzy and Jack in the booth. Other patrons sneaked from their cubicles, dashing for the safety of the dark alley beyond the exit. Distant sirens screamed as police cars approached the far end of the alleyway.

'When I tell you, both of you will get up and stand where I was standing. The Praha Police shoot first and interrogate afterwards. You two will be my …'

'Shield,' said Suzy.

'Yes. Thank you. You will be my shield. Now, stand up and slowly move around this side.'

As they circled one way, he circled the other. Jack was white and visibly shaking.

Gregor placed the pistol on the table, pulled his wife's left hand up, and removed her rings. He discarded all except the engagement ring and carefully wiped it off, gazing into the central diamond. He picked up the gun again, loosely holding it in his right hand, allowing the table to take its weight.

'She wouldn't return this ring, although she defiled it,' Gregor said in a vague tone of self-justification for his actions.

'But,' asked Suzy hesitantly, 'you didn't kill them both for the value of a ring—surely it was not so simple—perhaps for her betrayal?'

'Both! The engagement ring was my mother's, so it has a special value to me, far beyond money—But yes, mainly for her betrayal. And Viliam's treachery as well.'

They could hear movement in the alleyway, and several small front windows tinkled inwards as the police sought to reconnoitre the situation inside.

'We could negotiate with the police for you? One of us could stay here with you and the other ...'

'Ne! Ne!' said Gregor angrily. Then he added in a softer tone, 'I'm sorry, this is not your problem.'

'With a crime of passion—you may receive consideration—less time in prison,' said Suzy.

'My life is already a prison. Imprisoned in a thankless institution; imprisoned in a loveless marriage. I could escape neither and keep my honour—I come from a proud and honourable family—I could never accept incarceration.'

He was silent again. While Suzy patiently waited, Jack's fingernails were nervously digging into her arm. Suzy shook herself free of him.

Eventually, Gregor continued, 'I cannot surrender. Viliam, Gretchen's wastrel lover, is my supervisor at the department. They conspired to steal my report on the modernisation of our section, and he was to be promoted, while I would remain a grade three civil servant. Last night, when I told Gretchen, she just laughed. She said I was a failure, with no money and no future, and that she was leaving—for good this time—with Viliam.'

Tears trickled down his face.

'Hannah, her sister, encouraged her. They are no more than harlots, and I should've known.'

'But what will you do now?' asked Suzy.

'I know what I must do now,' Gregor replied.

His eyes closed; he was exhausted and silent. The entrance door behind Suzy and Jack creaked slowly inwards, and then, simultaneously, the lights in the bar went out and a powerful searchlight, directed from the alleyway outside, lit up their corner. They could now see nothing beyond their small circle.

Gregor was no longer a grim, sinister figure in silhouette, grotesquely under-lit by a flickering table lamp, but handsome, clean-shaven, and well dressed in a business suit and striped tie.

'You will stand in front of—what is your name?' he asked Suzy.

'I am Suzy—this is Jack.'

'Jack, you will stand behind Suzy and grip her arms.'

Jack, his face drained of blood, wordlessly obeyed.

'Jack, when I say so—you will both go to the floor—very quickly?'

Jack nodded but said nothing.

'*Ne! Gregor, ne!*' begged Suzy.

He smiled at hearing the exact words Gretchen had used earlier, but this time the tone was soft and pleasing, friendly, filled with a genuine feeling for him.

'Suzy. You will hold out your hand—pleez?'

He placed the diamond ring in her hand and then closed her fingers around it.

'*Dekuje Gregor*—thank you,' she said. Tears trickled down her cheeks.

He calmly removed the ammunition clip from the gun and placed it on the table of their booth.

'Now, Jack! Now!' whispered Gregor. As Jack dragged

Suzy down, Gregor quickly stood up, swinging his harmless gun upward, pointing it towards the state police, invisible behind the klieg lights.

'*Na shledano Gregor*,' whispered Suzy, lying on the cold floor.

Gregor heard her say goodbye just before the clattering machine guns threw his shattered body against the blood-stained brick wall.

The bar was silent.

Suzy, sobbing on the blood-smeared cobblestone floor, opened her shaking hand and tiny blue shafts of light flickered from the diamond, reflecting its brilliance even in the dim light. Blue and yellow fingers radiated outwards as if from a little glitter ball. Jack reached for her hand, but she pushed him away.

The police closed in on the table behind protective shields, their guns drawn, shouting in Czech for them to get their hands up. Suzy said, 'When we get back to our pension, you can pack your bag and leave. I don't ever want to see you again. But first, I want to explain to the police what really happened here. And if Gregor has family, tomorrow I want to find them and tell them what a fine man he was.'

EVIL EYE

I WAS LOOKING FORWARD to my second boat trip scuba diving with the Mount Underwater Club even though I had ended up in the Hyperbaric Chamber in Auckland after my first trip, proving that no matter how fit and skilled you are, you need the right gear. So I took out a student loan at the Polytech to buy a new wetsuit, buoyancy compensator, mouthpiece and regulator, a speargun, and two bottles. The loans have no interest charges while you are still studying, so I took out some extra because it's great to have savings in the bank and some cash for a beer on Friday nights.

The speargun was a beaut: French made, double rubbers, and a long reel of heavy line for spearing kingies. It even had a built-in bungee rubber as a shock absorber for when you hit a really big one. So I practised deep breathing at my flat so that I could hold my breath longer underwater. But you have to be careful doing that; after about a dozen deep breaths, I keeled over on the floor, my eyes rolled back in their sockets, and I started shaking uncontrollably. The two girls at the flat immediately started screaming. I could sort of hear them in the background, if you know what I mean. While one dialled 111 for an ambulance, the other ran some cold water in a pot and threw it in my face. That sure brought me back to life, the cold water running down inside my clothes.

The girls had asked me to leave the flat several times for various reasons and seemed a little surprised—almost disappointed—that I survived, spluttering and coughing as I struggled to my feet. I got a towel and was drying myself when we heard the siren of the ambulance. Two burly fellows leapt out and pushed past Sharlene, who had opened the door to tell them they were no longer needed. They threw me on the stretcher and threatened to strap me down if I didn't stop struggling. Eventually, I convinced them I was alright. They went away very unhappy because I think it affected their job performance reviews if they failed to transport a patient to the prescribed destination.

So Sunday arrived, and we travelled by the Manutere out to Tuhua Reef. I sat calmly on the boat going out, waiting for the first dive and thinking how great it would be to shoot a big kingie. We all geared up, me in my new dive gear, and everyone else buddied into pairs. A couple of divers offered me the chance to make it a threesome with them, but I calmly said I was just going to mooch around the reef and see what I could see. Fred, who had previously dived with me, was on board but seemed to be avoiding me. He gave me the evil eye a couple of times and mumbled something to the club captain, but I won't repeat that here—just in case children read this story.

I took up my speargun and jumped overboard. I equalised my weight with a few squirts of air, paddling towards the rock. It was good: the visibility, the swirling kelp, and most of all, the fish life. Demoiselles, maomao, and tiny little smelt with yellow fins, all swarmed this way and that, shining in the sunlight. The water fizzed up in front of me, so I discharged air from my BC. I slowly descended below the broken water and swam on towards the rock. I got down to about fifteen metres, and the main reef appeared in front of me. Only a few metres below me, I saw a pinnacle, tall and slim and sticking up like a stalactite, or is it stalagmite, so I dipped lower to pass it. This was cruisie, surrounded by all the fish I had seen on posters.

Suddenly, out of the gloom, I saw the kingies coming in, straight for me it seemed, but they veered away at the last possible moment and circled me and the pinnacle.

'Blast,' I thought, 'I haven't loaded the gun yet.' So with a bit of grunting, I got the two rubbers clicked onto the notches of the spear. As I armed the gun, I had settled a little deeper and came to rest at the base of the pinnacle about twenty metres deep. The kingfish, interested in watching me arm the speargun, were still circling me and the rocky spire. As I stood upright and took a bead on each fish, it moved around and out of my aim before I could fire. But the largest fish seemed more curious and paused as I pointed the spear, so I closed my eyes and fired.

When I opened my eyes, what I saw next was amazing. The spear had pierced the big fish near the base of its tail, and it took off like a rocket. The other kingies in the school exploded outwards in panic and raced away. I gripped my speargun fiercely as the big fish ran out the reel of line. The bungee insert in the cord twanged tight and, the fish veered to the left. I turned to watch, but it disappeared behind the pinnacle because it was swimming in the circle determined by the length of the cord attached to the spear. I then saw the big kingie reappear on the other side of the pinnacle, still swimming with awesome power in a full circle. It was less than half my weight but seemed to have ten times my strength as it passed in front of me.

The fish seemed to be staring at me with the one evil eye I could see. I froze with excitement at my success.

'I've got him! I've got him!' I shouted aloud to myself. Thinking back, I'm not sure who realised it first—me or the fish—but it had got me too, as the first loop of the cord passed over the gun and both my arms and wrenched me up against the pinnacle. After the second pass, the fish was two metres closer to me, and that evil eye seemed a lot nearer, and I was bound more tightly against the pinnacle. Even though I was stationary and the fish was swimming away from me as fast as it could go, I realised that the fish and I were actually on a collision course. Before I could divide the length of the cord by the radius and multiply by pi, to work out how many circles it had left, the fish had looped me again.

It was soon terrifyingly close. The big eye focussed on me. A flash of thought passed through my mind, do fish believe in utu? Was it intent on revenge? Tied rigidly against the pinnacle, I could no longer reach my knife to cut the cord to free this demon fish. During the next pass, even quicker, because the joining cable was getting shorter and shorter, I could feel the swirl of water from the big beating tail fin. I could have reached out and touched it, but I was trussed up like a Christmas turkey. The fish crashed against me and thrashed and flapped there until it stunned itself against the rocky pinnacle.

I soon realised I was wastefully chuffing out through the mouthpiece with my excited breathing and slowed down to conserve air. The demoiselles and maomao came back and surrounded me, totally without fear. An angelfish swam by, and I wondered whether it was a good omen or perhaps a fish's way of farewelling humans.

Fred had seen the burst of bubbles from the boat and decided to swim over to investigate and plunged down towards me. He gestured as if asking me if I wanted to be released. I could still nod despite the rings of cord binding me to the rock. But he shook his head with a wicked laugh; his look made me think again of the fish's big evil eye, intent on utu. I was very relieved when I realized he was just joking. I wondered for a minute whether he would, after our earlier experience diving together. He even helped me get the big kingie back to the boat.

ME TOO!

I COULD TELL they were mother and daughter; both were fair-haired, but not bottle-blonde; and about the same height, maybe five foot six. They were all class! Either would turn a man's head, but neither was the sort that would deliberately walk past a building site if you know what I mean. If they did, I'm sure their response to a wolf-whistle would be to smile inwardly at the compliment but show no outward sign.

I met them at a dive resort called Galapagos Inn, on the Isle of Cozumel, off the coast of Yucatan Peninsula in southeast Mexico. I happened to be sitting at the adjacent table at breakfast, eating *huevas revoltas,* a delicious plate of sautéed red and green peppers in scrambled eggs when I recognised the soft kiwi accent of my own country. As I had my coffee and they waited for their order to arrive, I couldn't help overhearing that they had something else in common: both had recently split up. The older woman's husband had run off with a younger woman about a year earlier, and the daughter, who was about my age, had just had a row with her partner.

The daughter had decided to come across to Mexico to look at the Aztec ruins and do a scuba course, leaving a bitter New Zealand winter behind. I travelled in the reverse direction: visiting Mexico on my way home after several years working in the States. The mother had come with her daughter to keep her company. She was less worried about her departed husband, whose mind had been elsewhere for some years.

I heard Christal say to her daughter, 'Helena, your father's dolly bird still manages to convince him that she yearns for his worn-out body and incisive wit.' They laughed, quite relaxed with each other.

When we queued to enrol for the scuba course, I was behind them. The younger woman filled out and signed the waiver form. Stefan, the instructor, was tall, half-Spanish, half-Mexican, and had a pleasant, accented voice—deep and mellow—belying his slim build. He looked to be in his mid-forties. As he smiled and bent over to sign off the documentation, the younger woman, almost imperceptibly, raised her eyebrows at her mother in mock admiration. The instructor zapped her credit card in payment, after which Helena turned to leave—but her mother remained at the counter.

'Me too!' she said.

'*Perdoneme la senora?*' queried the instructor.

'I wish to do the course too,' she responded.

'Christal! What are you doing?' asked Helena.

'I said I would come with you. And that is what I intend doing,' was the reply. Christal raised her eyebrows in imitation of her daughter, who shrugged in amusement and waited while her mother enrolled.

Later in the morning, about a dozen of us attended the theory session of the course, learning about the change in pressures deeper down, the need for a buoyancy compensator and a weight belt, and how they helped control our descent and ascent. Stefan explained to us all the signals and safety procedures. His resonant voice was reassuring, instilling confidence in the class. Both the New Zealand women seemed to absorb all the information, occasionally asking a question, which Stefan answered.

Among the group was a young American woman who talked nearly as much as Stefan. Her know-it-all comments were laced with double-entendre. She seemed to be laying claim to the instructor's full attention, not just for scuba training. It all seemed to go over Stefan's head until near the end of the lesson, when he explained that resort staff members were forbidden from making passes at their clients, no matter how tempted they may be! The women in the class sighed in good-humoured disappointment, especially the American. Stefan was a pretty smooth operator, quite able to defuse unwanted attention with such good grace.

Early in the afternoon, we geared up by the small rock

pool with a short tunnel leading out to the bay in front of the resort. Stefan and his female assistant checked our equipment, making sure we were comfortable in the bulky gear. They took us down into the pool one by one, helping us to do a few laps submerged beneath the surface as we familiarised ourselves with the scuba gear. They led us through the tunnel to the sea, where they swam with us gradually down to about 25 feet. After getting used to the scuba equipment and the alien environment, we came back through the tunnel. Most of the new divers were nervously excited during this experience; the American woman was loud, squealing, and volubly disappointed that the female instructor took her on her swim. Christal seemed very reluctant and held back until last. Stefan took her into the pool more slowly than the others. They surfaced once, and he explained again how the buoyancy controls worked. She looked over at the rest of us in slight embarrassment before they disappeared down the tunnel together.

Our class re-grouped after a coffee break, boarded the dive boat, and travelled out to the reef for our first dive. The boat was about 10 metres long, the gunwales about a metre off the water, and we sat all geared up around the edge.

The American woman shrieked, 'Go the US Marines!'

Stefan briefed us on how to roll back off the gunwales into the sea, dropping to about 40 feet deep and how the current would take us slowly across the reef structure while the boat drifted above, the boatman following our bubbles. He reassured the party that he or his assistant would be with us every instant in the water. Starting with Christal, he reached out, touching her on the forehead and saying, 'Go,' and Helena watched in amazement as her mother obediently rolled backwards into the open ocean. Despite their apprehension, everyone else copied the courage of the oldest of their party.

We drifted downward in the water, gathering on a sandy patch of the floor of the Caribbean, just as a group of large fish swam by, totally unperturbed by our intrusion. We each made an OK sign with forefinger and thumb held together, forming a circle. Stefan came into the group and took Christal's hand in his own and led the phalanx of swimmers away, half swimming, half drifting, towards the reef, his female assistant as a safety lookout above and behind us. Stefan pointed out a colossal wrasse as it turned and swam over to inspect us. We stopped by the reef, and he pointed out brain coral, fan coral, bucket sponges so big a person could have hidden inside one, and a king crab as large as a dinner plate that reared up on its hind legs anticipating an imagined attack. Fish of all colours and sizes ignored us as we drifted past. He took us behind a shaded cliff and showed us a nest of painted lobsters, facing into the current with their feelers swaying to and fro.

Suddenly, Stefan bunched his free hand into a fist, indicating danger, and slowed everyone down while a sizeable grey sand shark cruised past about five metres away. Christal pressed in close beside Stefan until the ugly beast had passed. Later, Stefan indicated a swim-through a little deeper, and we all bombed downwards into the shade of the hole, through the beautiful multi-coloured tunnel, and out again into the diffused sunlight. He then pointed to the boat above, and we made a slow controlled ascent and boarded, still in awe at our time below in another world. The 40 minutes had passed so quickly it seemed like only 10.

Back at the resort, I was having a coffee with Helena and Christal when she told her mother she was dining that evening with a few other divers. Christal smiled warmly at us as she replied, ‘I’m not blind, you know.’

‘Yes,’ I said, ‘I organised the dinner. There’s a nice Mexican restaurant called el Paradiso in town, so I asked Helena and a few other divers and booked a table. What about you Christal, What are your plans? Would you like to join us?’

‘Oh, yes! Me too! I am going to *el Paradiso,* but I’m going with Stefan!’ replied Christal.

‘I’m not blind either, Mother. But didn’t Stefan say he’s not allowed to make passes at his clients?’ Helena’s challenge was pretty neat, and she added a raised eyebrow in mock disapproval of her mother.

But Christal’s response was neater still, ‘Oh no! Stefan never made a pass at me; I invited him!’

FISHING TIME

AT THE FUNERAL SERVICE, the fishing club president gave a pleasant enough eulogy about Richard, but his words missed the essence of the man. In fact, the president almost denigrated Richard with faint praise, mentioning that he'd led a simple life, never owned his own boat, but had been held in high regard by his fellow members as a good club man. The president thought he knew Richard well, but his shallow view never described the real Richard. He expressed sympathy about Richard's ongoing heart condition but did not comment on what I believed to be Richard's unique gift. Overall, the president's half-hearted words disappointed me.

It didn't surprise me that no one who spoke at the funeral service mentioned Richard's eye for beauty: his appreciation of the patterns he saw in nature. He would point out to me the brilliant rippled hues of cirrus clouds on the dawn horizon; spirals of sea birds rising and falling and streaming away above the island at the harbour entrance; the iridescent metallic colours of a freshly caught snapper as they turned in the light. His appreciation of such things—and sharing them with me—was what formed the bond between us.

His only son, Fergus, who had worked for years on oil rigs in Alaska and the North Sea, made a rare visit home for Richard's funeral and afterwards asked me to have a beer with him. I had met him quite a few times over the years and had always found him sullen and unfriendly, an immense disappointment to me. I had asked him to come fishing with me a few times, but he always turned me down.

After the service, like most of Richard's mates, we went to the clubrooms to commiserate and, as we entered, I pointed out Richard's name on the Honours Board. Fergus, who had been silent in the car, paused, looked at his father's name and nodded. He had become a man of even fewer words than Richard.

I wondered if he was as shallow as he seemed or if he had some unfathomed depth of feeling. While I bought a couple of beers, Fergus found a leaner in an unoccupied corner.

I sat the handles of beer on the leaner.

Fergus picked up his ale and said, 'Richard!'

'Richard!' I replied, and we both took a long draft of the amber liquid.

Fergus was tall and tanned, his physical strength evident even beneath a new suit bought for the funeral. Fergus had no resemblance to my mate Richard, who had been slight and short, although I could sometimes discern some of his mother's features in Fergus' symmetrical face.

Fergus turned to me and said, 'Of all his acquaintances, you knew Richard best.' It was not asked as a question or a matter for debate but stated as an indisputable fact.

'I suppose that's true,' I replied.

'And yet you never spoke at the service today?' queried Fergus.

'No,' I replied, a little worried that I may have offended him.

Fergus was about my height and glared at me across the leaner, and I felt compelled to justify myself: 'Richard and I were great fishing mates, and I've never been much of a public speaker. I'll miss him now; what more could I have said?"

Fergus seemed dissatisfied with my answer, and it forced me to carry on, 'What mattered between us was not for others; it was private.'

'Even from me?' he countered.

'Even from you!' I said, trying to sound casual.

Fergus changed his mood abruptly and smiled slyly: 'You were great mates! Why was that?' He sipped on his beer, his eyes fixed firmly on mine, again compelling an answer.

'When I was bogged down in my business with more work than I could handle, Richard gave me a piece of advice. He was the costing manager in a large furniture manufacturing company. He told me to gradually increase my prices until the volume of my orders matched the time I wished to work. At first, I thought it too simple to be good advice, but I had doubled my monthly income before long and had time to go fishing again. When I thanked him, he suggested I put in a showroom and stock a range of the most popular fabrics, not just for tarps and canopies that I manufactured but also furniture fabrics. He said to visit all the other operators in my line of business and offer them generous discounts on fabrics they purchased from me. The mark-up on those lines was so good that my net income doubled again.'

'And so, in exchange for that advice, you never let him pay you when he went fishing on your boat, and when he was sick or stuck for cash, you helped him out.' Again, it was a statement from Fergus rather than a question.

'In my book,' I said, 'he was well ahead on favours. And anyway, I enjoyed fishing with him.'

Fergus nodded, and we both sipped our beer. I felt I was getting to know him a little better. He seemed black and white in his opinions, but I sensed something was driving him.

'You knew Richard was not my birth father?' stated Fergus.

'Yes,' I said, concerned at the direction of our conversation.

'What I think upset him most was my mother's betrayal,' stated Fergus.

'You'd be right,' I said but did not elaborate.

'Richard never found out he was not my birth father until I was at secondary school,' said Fergus. 'My mother, in a fit of fury one night, spilt it all out. She told him he might have been clever on business matters but was boring and that she was leaving with someone she had just met.'

I nodded.

'And if they had just met—then obviously he was not my birth father?'

'No, I suppose not,' I replied.

Fergus began to fidget. 'She refused to say who my father was. She refused then and has ever since, and I haven't seen her for years. My mother was a bit of a—how should I put it nicely—with men, she had a short attention span.'

'Yes, I reckon so,' I said. 'But your mother was lovely—and Richard loved her—despite all her faults—even after she left him. It was all about age, you know, and being with Richard made her feel old.'

'Strange, I think I must have done the same,' said Fergus, 'A bit hard pretending you're 35 when your son is 31.'

I laughed, but Fergus looked out the windows at the still, dull-blue water of the harbour that carried the reflection of the far off hills.

Then turning and looking straight into my eyes, he said, 'What about you? How did you feel about my mother?'

I could sense the rising colour in my cheeks. I started to speak, stopped, and after a long pause, I said, 'I loved her too—very much.' My voice faltered, faded, and froze.

Fergus' eyes were like gimlets, hard and penetrating.

Then with my courage stripped of confidence, 'If Richard never knew, how come you guessed?'

'Each time, over the years—when you asked me to go fishing, I became a little more convinced—mainly by your increased disappointment, each time I refused,' replied Fergus.

This time I was dumbfounded, and it was Fergus who continued. His eyes became softer, his mouth relaxed in a half-smile, 'I'm here for a few more days. Does that offer to go fishing still stand?'

SHAG POINT

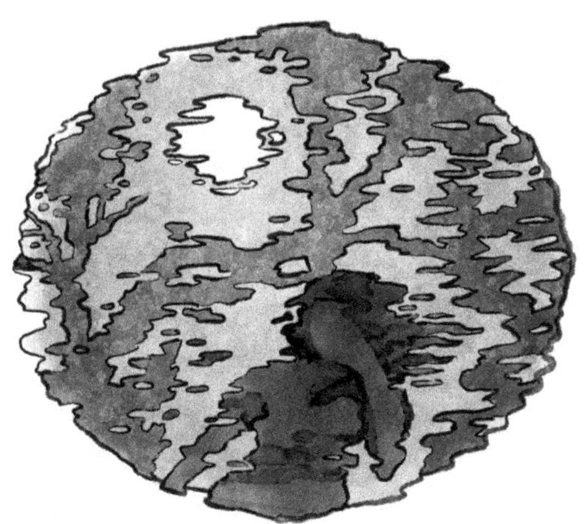

AS THE BOAT entered the cutting, the two men stood on the transom, pissing into the foaming wake. They had been chatting about previous great fishing competitions on the island and their regret when the island's owner discontinued them a few years earlier. Hemi was the licensed skipper of the charter boat, a tall, heavily-built man, his brown face lined from the combined effects of worry and exposure to the sun. Howie was an earthmoving contractor, Hemi's only customer that day. He was short, sandy-haired and seemed laconic, but Hemi knew from earlier trips Howie could be decisive when necessary.

Hemi's teenaged son, Shane, was at the helm and throttled back as he'd seen his father do many times. Shane was proud of the trust his father was beginning to show in him as a deckhand. He knew it was a means for his father to save wages for a proper deckie since the steady downturn in his charters over the last few years. As they approached the jetty, Hemi took over again, spun the wheel hard and shoved the controls into reverse. The 40-foot launch eased quietly against the rubber bumpers on the pier. Howie leapt onto the timber deck with the bow rope, and the lad tied the stern onto the base of the jetty sign that read: Cormorant Resort—Private Landing—Keep Off.

Hemi said, 'You wash up, kid! I got serious stuff to talk with ya mum.'

It didn't worry Shane; another chance to show he could do the job. He ran the hose out as the two men ambled up the path, passing the barely legible, handwritten sign, rotting and half-covered by weeds and long grass, that read: *Welcome to Shag Point*. At the fork in the path, Hemi turned up to the modest house among the trees, and Howie walked on towards the buildings further up.

Sitting on deckchairs in the early evening light were the owners of the property. Clifford wore dark sunglasses, a green reefer jacket with a pocket embroidered with a Latin motto beneath an eagle. Lindy wore a light blue sun frock, the same colour as her bright blue eyes. She had a plain cream golf shade to protect her face from the sun, and her light leather belt was the same shade as her sandals. Glasses of wine sat on the small table.

'So you caught some fish, old boy?' With Clifford's BBC accent, he sounded like a British aristocracy member, yet he'd been born in Timaru. He sometimes bragged that his father had been Mayor of that small city and later was elected as the local Member of Parliament for a single three-year term.

'Quite a few nice snapper,' said Howie. 'I gave some to Hemi and thought Lindy might cook some for us.'

'We have eye-fillet on the menu tonight, but Lindy will freeze your fillets,' said Clifford. 'And that includes any fillets that Hemi's taken. I've told him before: any fish caught belong to the customer.'

'No problem about Hemi,' said Howie. 'The fillets were mine—I gave them to him—now they're his—no big deal. And fish is better fresh than frozen.'

'I haven't taken the steak out of the freezer yet, and I'm happy to cook your fish later,' said Lindy, standing up and taking the tray of fillets from Howie. 'Would you like vegetables or a salad with your fish?'

'A salad sounds fine,' said Howie, smiling.

'Would you like the fish crumbed?'

'That sounds nice.'

Clifford frowned with disapproval as his wife vanished inside the house.

'I might have a shower,' said Howie, and he wandered down the row of small separate units that constituted Cormorant Resort. As he stripped off his shirt, he made a call on his cell phone.

'All signed up then, and the deposit banked?' He smiled to himself as he dropped his trousers. 'Legally enforceable? Okay, thanks. Enjoy your evening.'

He showered quickly and arrived back on the verandah in casual slacks and an open-necked shirt.

Clifford was there with a replenished glass: 'Marlborough savvy, a classy white, old chap? Nice year this one—2020, I think—like a glass?'

'No, but I'd love a beer,' said Howie, noticing Lindy inside, busy in the kitchen.

'Steinlager or Heineken?' asked Clifford as if there were only two beers worthy of the name.

'Heineken,' responded Howie.

Clifford reappeared with the opened bottle and glass.

'Don't pour it,' said Howie, taking only the bottle and waving the glass away. 'Cheers, pal,' he said and took a slow swig from the bottle.

'Good health,' said Clifford, raising his glass and sipping his wine.

After the sun went down, the three of them, Clifford, Lindy, and their guest, Howie, shifted to a larger table inside the French doors, overlooking the moonlit sea. In the pohutukawa trees, near the jetty, a colony of pied shags noisily settled into their roosts for the night. Lindy had made an appetiser of mussels and avocado. Howie slipped back to his unit and returned with a bottle of bubbly from the fridge.

'So, what's the occasion?' asked Lindy.

'I have just had an important contract accepted.'

'Before you celebrate, you should make certain it's legally watertight,' said Clifford. 'We've had some tyre-kicker looking at this place over recent months, but he's been all show and no dough! Just some jerk trying to rip us off.'

'What was your contract, Howie?' asked Lindy, trying to change the subject.

But Clifford, with at least three glasses of wine in him, was irrepressible, 'We've developed this place as much as it can be. You must know that Howie—you've been coming here each year a couple of extra times lately. We've refurbished every unit: brand new furniture—redecorated throughout—even renovated the kitchen and restaurant areas. We changed the name from Shag Point to Cormorant Resort. A fat lot of appreciation from the customers, though, tasteless bunch!'

'Steady on, Clifford,' said Lindy. 'Howie is our best customer—our only customer this week—and he's hardly tasteless, not to me at least.'

'Sorry, chum, no offence meant,' said Clifford. He poured a second glass of Howie's champagne for himself. 'But you have no idea how much blasted money I've poured into this dump. And yet, every month, for some reason, the visitor numbers drop. So now the market is down, and we can't quit it at any price. I detest this place!'

'So, where are you at with your sale?' asked Howie.

'When we finally agreed on the price, the buyer insisted Hemi sign up for a further five years as our charter skipper, and his wife as cleaner and gardener. Hemi and his wife agreed, but I can't stand the man—let alone her—and insisted that their new contract is subject to us achieving a final sale of the resort.'

'But it's a partnership,' protested Lindy. 'We need them, just like they need us.'

'The Hemis of this world are a dime a dozen,' snarled Clifford.

'So, what happened then?' asked Howie.

'Bizarre! The buyer's next move was absolutely bloody bizarre!' said Clifford. 'He insisted we sign individual employment contracts to stay on ourselves, but only at his option. That means he could keep me on, but sack Lindy.'

Lindy stood up suddenly to get the crumbed fish from the oven, but she paused when Howie spoke.

'Or vice versa?' asked Howie.

Howie silently watched her go, sensing she was upset. 'What?' said Clifford. 'Yes! Yes! I suppose he could sack me and keep Lindy on. But who'd manage the blasted place then?'

Lindy returned carrying a tray with a bowl of salad and plates of crumbed snapper. She sat the bowl between the men, who had fallen silent.

'Just help yourselves.' She smiled and gestured towards the tray. Her mood had changed. She moved around the table and, taking the champagne bottle from the bucket of ice beside Clifford, topped up the three glasses.

She sat down, now impatient, almost cajoling, 'Howie, are you going to tell us what we're celebrating tonight—or not?'

Howie remained silent as he held the salad bowl out to Lindy. She used the serving tongs to put salad on her plate beside the crumbed fish, but her inquiring eyes seemed to repeat the question. Howie held her gaze but avoided her question, holding the bowl now for Clifford, who seemed surprised at this change of role by their guest.

As they began eating, Howie asked, 'Has your buyer paid a deposit for your property?'

'Yes,' said Lindy, but Howie sensed she had now become remote and cold.

'According to my barrister,' said Clifford, 'the buyer can still back out in the next thirty days, but if he wishes to go ahead, we're committed to selling.'

'So your buyer has a legally enforceable option?' asked Howie.

Suddenly alert, Clifford stopped eating; Lindy was ominously silent.

'I'm the buyer,' said Howie quietly. 'I've sold my contracting business and can assure you I'm not just a tyre-kicker. But there are a few things we need to discuss, and I hope we can do so amicably.'

Clifford was flushed and angry. 'That's a bit bloody rich! Why the secrecy? Why not just discuss things with us—out in the open—between friends.' He stood up. 'You owe us an explanation.'

'It's just business,' replied Howie.

'Well, it's not how I have ever behaved in business—but it appears that the ball is entirely in your court—old boy.'

'That's not entirely true,' said Lindy, 'Some decisions I'll make for myself, in my own good time.'

'Fair enough,' said Howie.

'You've deceived us,' said Lindy. 'While you've been here pretending to fish, you've been poking around the property and checking out a good business deal for yourself—and …'

Lindy's face reddened. She stood up in confusion. Instead of stalking inside, as Howie had expected, she walked to the edge of the deck, looked down at the dark, brooding sea, and took the steps down towards the beach, leading away from the jetty. As she followed the track, she stopped and turned at a clump of flax. For a minute or so, she watched Howie and Clifford in earnest conversation.

Howie was making a vigorous chopping motion with his right palm; Clifford's chin was supported by one hand, his elbow on the table, beside his forgotten meal. Each time Howie stopped speaking, Clifford shook his head in disbelief. His shoulders slumped; Lindy felt the humiliation her husband was suffering. She left them to their discussions, still angry but feeling a mix of guilt and nervous excitement. When she reached the beach, she kicked off her shoes and walked in the sand above the water line for about a hundred metres, then sat on the low branch of a pohutukawa, a spot she regularly visited after any disagreement with Clifford.

She watched the incoming tide, the bulk of the surging sea spreading inwards, but on the crest of each breaking wave, an offshore breeze was whipping up a fine spray of water. After each wave had broken, the sea levelled out, forming ponds that reflected vague night images: shivering leaves, swaying tree ferns, scudding clouds and other unrecognisable movements. These confused elemental forces heightened Lindy's emotional state, and she began weeping quietly, knowing her life was now being ripped apart by influences beyond her control. She sympathised with Clifford but knew she didn't love him anymore. Her feelings for Howie oscillated between resentment and curiosity, resentment because of the sudden disruption he'd so callously planned and executed, mixed with an intense curiosity about his motives.

She stopped weeping and began walking further down the beach, towards the rocky point. She did not want to discuss or consider her future any further tonight. She deliberately rounded the point to be out of sight from the steps below the house. The tide was now full, and she sat on a rounded boulder near the waterline. After five minutes or so, she could see a figure on the beach walking around the point towards her, knowing from the profile it was Howie. She resigned herself to what must now occur.

'How did you know where I was?' she asked.

'I followed your footprints.'

'You must think I'm pretty stupid.'

'You know that's not what I think! And I thought you'd guessed I was the buyer long ago.'

Lindy didn't reply.

'Lindy, I've just told Clifford it's you I want to help me run the business, and he's resigned to leaving.'

'Do I have any say in this?' she asked, 'or is this some sort of coup-de-grace?'

'The decision on the sale is yours to agree or otherwise.'

'But you said you had a legally enforceable option?'

'If you're unwilling to stay and help, then I wouldn't enforce the contract. Instead, I'd simply step back from the purchase. That's what an option means.'

'There are other issues, though, aren't there? I haven't forgotten your attempt to—proposition me.'

'Proposition is a bit strong,' he replied. 'Lindy, you did show me through the house, and in the bedroom, all I …'

'You stood in the doorway to stop me leaving and told me …'

'How lovely you were! And I still think so.'

'And you put your arm around me too, didn't you?'

'Yes, and I kissed you on the cheek, but then you turned your lips away.'

'And I told you we shouldn't be doing these things.'

'Yes, but you didn't push me away or pull yourself free. And you still welcome me here, especially today, and you are always warm and friendly. I didn't get to tell you how much I wanted you.'

'I knew you wanted me, alright—but now I'm learning just how much. So how do we handle that issue? Or am I like the other fixtures and fittings, I come with the property?'

'If I had been open, I imagine my offer would have been instantly rejected, especially by you. However, Clifford still wants to sell, even if you choose to stay.'

'That doesn't surprise me. He wants out at any price, even if it includes leaving me behind apparently, like one of the chattels!'

'So much for love!' said Howie. 'So much for your ticking clock and starting a family!'

Lindy smiled, but it was a grim smile. 'I'd never have talked with you that day about my feelings if I'd known you'd pull a trick like this. That was a private conversation, and I didn't imagine you'd ever use it against me like this.'

'You're right, Lindy, I'm sorry, but this is still a private conversation. So let's handle some things as they arise. There'll be no pressures from me, no surprises, no secret agendas.'

Howie paused, but Lindy remained silent. 'Clifford said you own half the equity here. I knew that anyway from the company and property records. So if things work out here—with the business—and with us—you could buy back your half at the same price as you've sold it.'

'And if it doesn't work out?'

'You'll have made a sale, received a fair price for your half, and you'll be free to go.'

Lindy was silent for a full minute, looking down into the reflections at her feet. When she spoke, her tone was mock-serious, almost facetious, but her warm smile of earlier in the evening had returned. 'Howie, you haven't even told me my salary, have you?'

'There'll be no salary—for either of us—but after a trial of twelve months, you will get half of any profits—whether you stay or go. But I believe we can make this place work—together!'

Lindy had become pensive again. 'I know this can be a good business. Clifford has worked very hard—but he's such …'

'Let's not go there,' interrupted Howie. 'Clifford has just told me that your lives together here had followed the same path as your business affairs.'

'That's true enough, I think he wants to go back to Timaru, but I don't! More to the point, what makes you think you can save this business?'

'I would talk everything through with you first, but I want to reinstate the fishing tournaments—and the Shag Point name! I would cut walking tracks over the property, plant native trees and remove the old pines. I would buy traps and exterminate the rats, stoats, feral cats, and magpies to encourage native birdlife. You know there are herons over the other side and tui and native pigeons as well as fantails. We could attract day visitors and overnight school groups. We would discuss everything together—and I wouldn't tell you or our guests what to cook! We could make salads and let them barbecue their fish or sausages or whatever with us on the house deck or at their units.'

Lindy looked up directly into Howie's earnest face. 'How long do I have to think about—I was going to say your proposition, but I won't use that word—how long do I have to think about your ideas?'

'As long as you need, but I hope you've already decided.'

When she spoke, it was quietly, 'I may have, but I'll tell you tomorrow morning after I've spoken with Clifford.'

ABOUT TWO

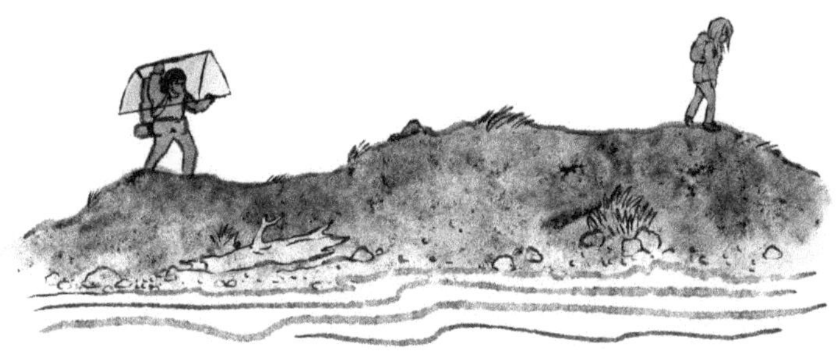

SHARON FIRST MET Frank on the learners' slope on the Whakapapa ski-field on Mount Ruapehu. She was just standing there on her skis, resting after practising elementary turns, and felt good about how much she had learnt. He came whizzing down in a half-crouched posture, and because of his total lack of skiing skills, was unable to avoid her. When he crashed into her, he grabbed her, and they slid together over the edge into a basin of soft powdery snow; Frank had collapsed on top of Sharon with their poles and skis sticking up like a pincushion as the falling snow gently covered them over.

When she opened her eyes and found herself trapped beneath him with their faces nearly touching, she realised what had happened, and she saw his clumsiness was only physical.

Frank said to her, 'You have lovely blue eyes.'

'And you can get off me, right now!' she replied angrily. 'You've just ruined my morning.' He helped her up and offered her a cup of coffee at the café. They found they both came from Palmerston North; she worked for an insurance company, and he was in his final year at Massey University.

After going to the movies a few times and getting on reasonably well, Frank suggested they go whitebaiting at the mouth of the Rangitikei River. It was spring, and the whitebait season had just opened. His brother had a set-net, and Frank had his tramping tent. He suggested they camp over on Saturday night to ensure they got a good position on the river at first light on Sunday morning. Sharon knew even less than Frank about fishing but agreed it could be fun.

So late on Saturday afternoon, with their packs on and wearing warm jackets and with Frank crouched under the wire and fabric net, they set off from the car to walk the five or six kilometres to get to the southern side of the river mouth. Frank had a large tramping pack with a small billy swinging from a buckle, and Sharon had a smaller daypack. Frank's brother had explained that few people fished the south side, and there was a better chance of catching some of the white gold if you walked out near the mouth on the north side.

At first, they walked on the grassy bank, then on the boulder-strewn edge of the river. Soon the banks became mainly dunes. They saw other whitebaiters, some crouching patiently on prominences that stuck out into the flowing stream, but mostly the others were returning after their long day on the cold river bank.

'How'd you go?' Frank asked each as they passed.

'Not bad' or 'Okay', they replied secretively.

'Buggerall!' said one old fellow, struggling back across the stones.

'Only about two today,' said an old Māori woman with a scoop net. 'And I'm packing it in soon.'

'What do you mean, about two?' asked Frank pausing beside her. Amongst other things, he was studying maths and believed in exactness. 'You can have one, or two, or three whitebait, but you can't have about two!'

'About two kilos, silly!' said the old woman, and then smiling, she added, 'Aren't you two going the wrong way?'

'We are camping over,' replied Sharon.

'Mmm. You've got a long wait then. Could be good if it's a clear night,' said the Māori woman. 'There's a full moon tonight and high tide about two in the morning.'

'That's what we thought,' said Frank, pretending that was what he had planned.

At the next ridge of rocks that ran out into the river, they stopped, and Frank threw the net down and removed his pack. 'This looks a good spot. A bit like the one back there by the Māori woman,' he said decisively. 'We'll pitch the tent here and then make a coffee.'

'Maybe we'll catch about two,' said Sharon, tired from the walk but still in good humour.

They pitched the little tent at the base of the dunes, protected from the cold westerly sweeping in off the sea and up the river. Sharon lay their sleeping bags side by side on the airbed in the tent as it darkened, and Frank got his little gas cooker going and made coffee. While they grasped their hot mugs and sipped on the coffee, they could see gulls and shags diving for small fish. Occasionally they caught a glimpse of a fish jumping as if kahawai were feeding on the smaller fish in the estuary.

'It is so calm and idyllic. I'm glad we came,' said Sharon. Then after a pause, she asked, 'How come the whitebait swim up the sides of the river?'

'The current's too strong in the middle, and there are more predators out there. They use the tides, seeking shelter and resting when the tide is going out, and then when the tide turns, they swim in on it.'

'That makes sense,' she replied

They sat cross-legged in the tent while they heated baked beans for their toast. By the time the beans were hot, their toast was cold, but they still enjoyed their meal together. He was putting his tramping experience to good use, and her confidence in his knowledge and experience grew. He rinsed the dishes in the river and stacked everything back in his pack. He put both their packs inside the tent and carefully placed the whitebait net in the lee of the tent so it would not catch the wind and blow away. They climbed fully dressed into their sleeping bags, using the light of Frank's torch that he had hung on the tent pole between them. He switched off the flashlight, and they carried on chatting for a while, but after their long walk along the riverbank, they were soon asleep.

About eleven o'clock, Frank woke suddenly and could hear heavy, rasping breathing and, frozen with fear, listened intently. Sharon was right next to him and seemed very still and quiet.

'Is that you?' he whispered.

'Of course not,' she whispered tartly. 'I thought it was you.'

Frank slowly reached for the torch and carefully faced it towards the tent flap, and he flicked it on. It was hard to tell who got the biggest fright: Frank, who gasped in horror; Sharon, who screamed in terror; or the cow with its head stuck through the tent flap, seeing the sudden bright light and the noisy reaction of the human intruders it had been curiously inspecting.

The cow leapt backwards, raising its head as it went, taking the entire tent with it. The bovine beast backed rapidly away with the tent over its head like a huge blindfold, bellowing loudly and bucking like a rodeo bull as it tried to shrug off the tent. After prancing in circles a few times, it managed to get rid of the tent and charged off into the darkness. Sharon still lay shaking in terror in her sleeping bag while Frank tried to make light of it. 'Not something I've ever experienced before on a tramping trip,' he said.

After reclaiming the tent and re-pitching it, they tossed and turned, sleeping only in snatches. About 3 am Sharon awoke with a start. 'Yuk! I'm all wet!' she said. Frank had no idea what had happened as Sharon crawled across the airbed towards the tent flap. As her weight left the bed, the water flowed over to Frank, who was on the higher side, filling his sleeping bag with cold water. He followed her out the tent flap, wading on his hands and knees through the water.

From the light of the full moon, they could see that the tide had risen, and surrounded the tent and was lapping at the base of the dunes.

'I'm cold and wet and tired,' said Sharon. 'I think we should just go home.'

'I'll get your pack,' said Frank in resignation. He waded back out to the tent and fished out her smaller pack, now sopping with water. After it had drained the bulk of the water, he helped her put it on.

'You start walking, and I'll catch up.' He handed her the car keys.

As Sharon started, Frank retrieved his pack, packed the tent and pegs, pushed everything into his backpack, and hung the billy on the buckle. He waded out to get the net. Sharon was only visible as a fading silhouette in the distance by the time he was ready to go, but he could see she was striding a lot faster than she had the day before, obviously very anxious to get back.

When he got to the car, she was sitting in the passenger seat, and her coldness was not all from her tidal dipping. He silently roped the whitebait net to the roof rack, threw his pack in the back beside hers, and went to the driver's door, carrying the billy.

'I would make you a cup of tea,' he said, 'but everything's so wet.' He paused, 'Besides ...'

'Besides what?' asked Sharon sullenly.

'Besides ... the billy is full of whitebait.'

Her face lit up as she peered in at the mass of wriggling, tiny, transparent fish.

'They were in the net when I fished it out of the river,' said Frank.

'About two,' said Sharon, still looking into the billy, cheerful again, and laughing, 'maybe even three!'

FELIZ NAVIDAD

AS I KISSED CYNTHIA GOODBYE, I could see the apology in her eyes. She squeezed my hand. It was quite civilised, although we had not discussed ending our twelve months together. When it had come time for us to leave

Barcelona for Madrid, at the last moment, Cynthia chose to go scuba-diving with the others in Majorca. But I was sick of diving and didn't enjoy diving during the colder months. We had dived in the Red Sea at Sharm el Sheik, but we hadn't sailed up the Nile to see the ancient ruins; we had dived around several Greek Islands but hadn't seen the Acropolis; we had dived off the Costa Brava in Spain, but had only glimpsed some of the Gaudi buildings, and seen nothing of the Picasso and Miro museums. We had the opportunity to change our course slightly to view magma exploding from Mt Etna, but no one else was interested. And after each diving expedition, our samplings of the local wines and beers had been excessive.

'More fun diving in Majorca!' Cynthia had said, but I was determined to go to Madrid—I spoke their language and loved their food and wanted to spend more time in Spain.

After the long train trip from Barcelona to Madrid, I found the *pensione* where I had booked a room. It was on the third floor of an old stone building. The lift was out of order because workers were digging up cables in the street outside, and I carried my suitcase up the stairs. It was dark in the stairwell even though it was still daylight on a winter afternoon. At the end of the hallway, a pair of pigeons fluttered briefly at my intrusion, then settled back to their cooing and froing. The old lady running the *pensione* apologised about the lift and the lights, but I waved her apologies away.

'No problema, la senora!'

She smiled. *'Gracias! Muy simpatico, el senor.'*

The room was clean and comfortable. I intended to sleep there, make daily excursions into the city, or perhaps take the train to Segovia and Toledo. Anything except more diving—followed by another hangover!

Outside the Metro, an old man rattled a can under my nose. *'Feliz Navidad!'*

I reached for my wallet and gave him some coins, but a smiling Christmas greeting did nothing to ease my malaise. Before I closed my wallet, I glimpsed the snapshot of Cynthia: her sun-bleached hair so fine to touch, and her silky-smooth skin tanned from the summer we had spent together. Our passion for each other had been fierce, like a volcanic eruption. I had hoped it would never end. Seeing her image warmed me with memories. On the train journey from Barcelona, I had unfolded her letters from behind the photograph in my wallet and re-read them.

As I emerged from the Metro after a day at the Museo del Prado, the night sky glowed through the mist, a dull reflection of Madrid's Christmas lights. The Plaza Major was bleak, with a chilly winter evening breeze. A crowd of mainly Spanish families paid homage at a traditional nativity scene, while a few noisy young tourists were making fools of themselves taking selfies with Mary and the baby Jesus and the Three Wise Men. As the young people left the display, a group of pickpockets was at work, like silent seagulls hovering behind a fishing boat, waiting for the chance to swoop upon any pickings. Suddenly I realised they were targeting me. They worked as a team, not unlike a planned soccer move, and once I recognised the signs, I watched them more closely. Their leader had gone ahead; he would probably stumble into me. The other two formed a pincer movement; one would be the diversion, the other the dip. There was perhaps a fourth somewhere who would disappear into the crowd with my wallet. As I paused, so too did they, gazing about, waiting for me to move on. I stood there, pointing at each one, in turn, drawing their attention to my awareness. Two of the younger men scowled, but the older man smiled at my show-poker defence. He was about forty, with an olive complexion and jet-black, slicked-back hair, wearing designer jeans and a leather jacket. He looked away. The group abruptly dispersed and went on their way and me on mine.

I wandered for an hour or so through the streets, looking in shop windows and bars, and wondering what Cynthia was doing. I walked through an enclosed market with its aromas of cheeses, hams and wet fish, where stall vendors were frantically busy, serving their customers with friendly gusto. I paused to look at bins of live Spanish lobster, their pincers taped.

Later, finding myself back at the Metro entrance, I went down into the bowels of the earth and was rapidly shuttled to the station nearest my *pensione*. An old man hobbled onto the bottom step at the escalator base, then stumbled and nearly fell. He recovered his balance by using his walking stick as a third leg. His actions blocked the escalator's full width, but I was in no hurry, and those behind me showed no impatience. We rose steadily towards the street level above.

As the escalator flattened off at the top, the old man looked stable, but the transition from the moving step to the stationary floor cast him forward onto his knees, and I tumbled on top of him, forced onward by people behind me. Some pushed past me, some half-stumbled but kept going, while others turned and helped us to our feet. The old man hobbled off as I brushed myself down. When I looked up, near the exit was the leader of the pickpockets, smiling and pointing at me just I had earlier pointed at him. I put my hand down to touch my wallet and cursed all Spaniards.

When I passed him, he infuriated me further, jeering, '*Feliz Navidad!*'

I was relieved that most of my money was with my credit

cards and passport in a money belt, still securely in place. As I walked back towards the *pensione,* I became aware that my mood had lifted; my step had somehow lightened. I saw a sign for a tapas bar and thought I might have a drink and a snack. Behind the bar was a plaque saying: 'Ernest Hemingway did NOT drink here!' The barman brought me a glass of red wine and a complimentary plate of smoked squid rings. He seemed sullen as if he wanted to be somewhere else.

As I sipped my drink, I watched the barman clearing the bar counter with a damp cloth, swishing the rubbish of previous customers directly onto the sawdust-covered floor. The day's detritus was left there, accumulating underfoot for sweeping up at the close of business. It was a curious Spanish practice I had not seen elsewhere. After watching him for a while, I realised that the thieves, in a similar way, had swept away Cynthia's photograph and letters.

I had not noticed it at the time, but the cooling of our love had been gradual, like spreading magma, slowly changing from white-hot lava to a cold, barren wasteland. As the barman wiped the bar near me, I said, *'Feliz Navidad!'* And he returned my greeting and my smile.

CIRCLES

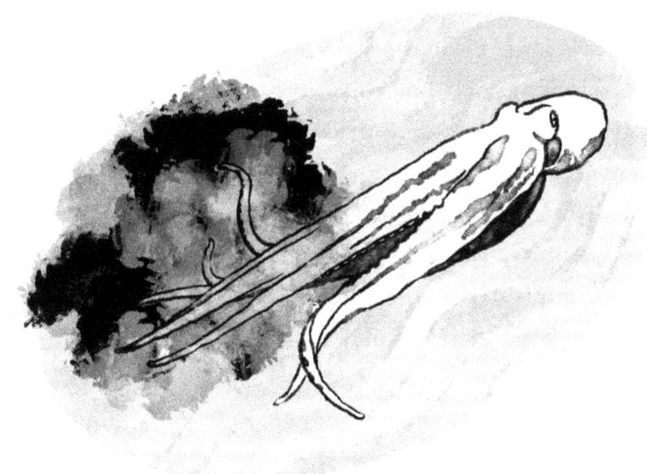

HE CLAMPED on his weight belt, flipped the backpack and bottle over his head, fixed the straps, and plunged over the side, finning down towards the seafloor, his muscular body spiralling down in the ecstasy of freedom. He was still angry about the failed search warrant, and he could've killed the cunning bastard for laughing at him when he opened up the cartons of old newspapers where he had expected to find electronic equipment. Since promotion to Assistant Inspector, his first big job and he'd stuffed it up, and he couldn't work out why.

The floor came up quickly. He missed the kelp-covered reef, and only silvery sand lay beneath. He did not mind swimming towards the shadowy outline of the reef. In front of him, a little mound of shells and stones surrounded a small hole, about 100 millimetres across. As he reached the mound, a murky blue-grey octopus, with tentacles streaming out behind, flowed out of the hole and raced towards the boulders, propelling her body with a pulsating jet-stream of water.

He stopped, curious, wanting to know what the octopus was up to, but his mind was still on the unsolved crime.

'Stop, look, and listen', his old boss in the CIB had said. 'and always listen to what the crims are thinking—not what they are saying.' How do you listen to what someone is thinking, for Christ's sake?

The octopus, nearing the rocks, swirled upward in a swooping curve, like a plane doing a deliberate aerobatic stall. The octi opened up like a parachute, splayed out in a sudden brilliance of redness against the blue-grey rock. The tentacles were spread their whole span of more than a metre, joined web-like near her body. Her large goggle eyes watched him. As he approached her, the octi settled on the rock, the redness dulling to brown; without moving, she vanished, becoming invisible, matching the rock's colour and texture. He wondered how an octopus did that because she could not see all of her own body, nor the rocks. Amazing!

He had been so sure a load of stolen electronic gear had been in the farm shed. That was where Wilson had been stashing his stuff for years. They had watched Wilson unload the cartons. Why the newspapers? Why bother?

He reached out to where he knew the octi had merged her colours with the rock. He thought he could see the narrow slits of her intelligent eyes. He touched the hard rock, then shifting his hand slightly, he could feel the softness of the octopus. She turned black in anger, jetting off again, leaving a cloud of black ink dispersing in her wake. He paddled up a little higher, above the murky darkness she had created and watched. He saw a grey slithering object near the next rock, a brief pause, then the octopus, sand-coloured, flowed across a patch of sand into the crevice of a kelp-covered rock, where she drew herself into a small cluster, looking much like the green kelp. When he approached, the octopus went white, knowing she had not fooled her potential predator.

He stood off a couple of metres and watched. He looked into the round goggle eyes. To ease her fear, he finned gently upward but still close enough to watch. Gradually, the animal returned to its blue-grey colour, and then the octopus lolloped across the sand like a big friendly Labrador, clearly aware the diver was still watching. She moved with two tentacles out each side as stabilisers, while two at the front pulled forward and the two at the back pushed, all eight working in harmony, and yet each carrying out different tasks. She had now traversed around in a circular path, and she flopped back into the hole from which she had initially emerged. The last two tentacles were left protruding as they scooped up shells and pebbles and shuffled them around, covering and disguising her lair. She withdrew the last tentacles, and the hole and the octi itself ceased to be visible, her eggs still safe inside her sanctuary!

He paddled back to the boat's anchor rope with most of the air still left in his scuba tank.

Back on board the boat, he pulled his cell phone from his dive bag and punched in some numbers with his still wet hand. 'Yeah, me here—tonight we do the same place again—Yeah, Wilson can scream harassment if he likes—just you and me though—not a word to anyone else—won't be newspapers tonight, it'll be stolen satnavs, fishfinders and other electronic stuff.

How do I know?—I have a theory—involves circles—yeah, that's right, circles.'

LONG ODDS

RUSTY WOULD BET ON ANYTHING! When he was fishing, he would have a series of bets with all and sundry. Each fishing trip was like a mini-tournament: first fish caught, the oddest, the best overall, and so on. In rugby, he would back either side depending on how many points he could negotiate. But Rusty was no gambling addict; he had never taken a Lotto ticket in his life, never visited a TAB, and was scathing about 'scratch and win', saying it was for mindless fools.

At first thought, this might seem an odd contradiction but, it was logical because he gambled with his fishing mates for social contact rather than money. That is not to say he didn't care about the result. Indeed he did! His enjoyment was in the excitement, continually chasing the unknown and publicly tallying up whether he was in front or behind with any person or any event. Surprisingly, it was a cheap hobby because so many of his bets were one on one with no percentage being creamed off by a third party. Besides, chance itself dictated that he would win 50% of the time, and he probably did slightly better than that. His loud and boisterous gambling often made him the centre of attention; some saw him as a slightly mad gambler while others thought him a bit of a character. Either way, he enjoyed and fostered those public perceptions of himself.

He was very wary of oddball bets. He had been caught out at the clubrooms once by a smart guy known to everyone as Slick, who said, 'If I put my wallet on the floor, I'll bet you $10 you can't jump over it!' After Rusty accepted the wager, the wise guy put the wallet in the corner of the clubrooms where Rusty couldn't possibly jump over it. He never really forgave Slick because it was not a fair bet but a dirty trick, and besides, he did not enjoy being laughed at by his friends. Nevertheless, he paid the ten bucks; his reputation would have been ruined forever if he had reneged.

Rusty was always a starter for something new. He was in Aussie on Anzac Day and played 'two-up' at an RSL club and, after losing a hundred dollars learning how it worked, he made a couple of hundred dollars profit, and that was after paying for his drinks and having a slap-up dinner. Back in New Zealand at the clubrooms, he vividly described his Aussie adventure to his mates, saying it was more like cock-fighting in Indonesia, with a hell of a lot of yelling and screaming than coin-tossing in a civilised country. As Rusty told his story, he waved his arms back and forth, imitating the drunk Australian gamblers. He was a bit off-put by the smirking presence of Slick, who had ripped him off with his wallet trick.

When Rusty had finished his yarn, Slick said, 'I've got a good bet for any takers.' Rusty's mates all leaned forward to listen, but Rusty stood up to go to the men's room, partly because he needed to and partly to avoid contact with the trickster. But Rusty paused and listened to the proposed bet. Slick had a piece of A2 paper loosely rolled up with a rubber band around it, like a big blank poster. 'It goes like this,' he said, unrolling the piece of paper. 'I'll bet you $10 each that you can't fold this single piece of paper eight times.' He paused while they considered it. Rusty saw a couple of them reaching for their money as he wandered over towards the men's bathroom area.

When Rusty arrived back, he slid his jacket onto the shelf under the leaner. The poster-sized piece of paper was now a tight little wad of paper that had unsprung on the leaner. Slick had five ten-dollar notes in his hand that he had just won and was explaining the reason, 'You see, each time you fold the paper, it doubles in thickness, and it impossible to get eight folds, because you run out of paper. And, believe it or not, it doesn't matter how big the piece of paper, it is impossible.'

'Bullshit!' said Rusty.

'You can say bullshit if you like, but I notice you didn't put up any money,' replied Slick.

'I'm talking about not being able to fold any piece of paper eight times,' said Rusty. Slick put his five ten-dollar notes between them on the leaner and said, 'I've got fifty dollars that say you can't fold any piece of paper eight times.' Rusty stared at the money for a while, fidgeted a bit as if embarrassed by this turn of events, and said, 'If you give me two to one, I'll double your bet.' Rusty took out his wallet and put two 50-dollar notes on the leaner to prove he was serious. Slick looked at him slyly, believing Rusty was trying to bluff him out of the bet by increasing the 'stakes'. 'And when are you going to perform this miracle?' asked Slick sarcastically. 'Right after you put up!' said Rusty, his face deadpan. Slick looked at Rusty again for a few seconds, sorted through his wallet. 'Now, you said,' demanded Slick.

Rusty reached under the leaner for his jacket, opened it up, exposing an unravelled toilet roll and then folded in half over and over: 'Carefully unfold that, counting as you go!' Rusty's mates publicly unfolded the toilet roll across the width of the clubrooms, counting loudly in unison as if they were still at primary school.

Slick looked slack as Rusty folded the notes and slipped them into his wallet.

TEMPTATION

I KNEW ADAM WELL. We had free dived together many times, spearing fish and diving with scuba gear for crayfish. Occasionally we would meet up near the end of the dive, comparing our catches or checking our air gauges deep down, and each would carry on alone. If we didn't meet up or become separated again, it didn't bother us too much, and we simply surfaced and made our way back to the boat separately. Usually, I got back first because he was more economical on air use than me.

As a scuba diver and freediver, he had a few particular characteristics. He would shoot maomao or butterfish and be happy to take home a feed. If he got lucky and speared a snapper, he thought it was a bonus. Once he speared a big kingfish, but it wasn't a good headshot. The fish plunged deep and took his speargun, line, and float with it, wrenching it from his grasp, demonstrating its incredible power. He never saw the fish or his gear again.

He wasn't upset though, just saying, 'The big one tempted me, and I paid the price, that's all'. I suppose if Adam's had a vulnerability, he could be easily tempted.

The last dive, we had gone much like every other one. We went to about 25 metres and split off around a giant boulder, and I went to the left; he went to the right. I saw a couple of crayfish straight away, got one quickly, and the second as well, after a bit of a struggle. I veered towards a vertical face and worked along that for a while but had no luck. I headed back toward the same boulder, getting close to the red zone on my air gauge. Almost immediately, I saw Adam. He had circumnavigated the rock, and his bag seemed full of crays. He had his full quota of six. I knew none would be undersized or soft or in berry. He was good like that, sticking to the rules.

We signalled 'okay' signs to each other. I held up my air gauge, now a little into the red, and indicated I was surfacing. Adam pointed down to a hole at the boulder base and wiggled his fingers like cray feelers, and spread his two palms wide apart—exaggerating the size. I laughed to myself, leaving him to it, and slowly surfaced, using up the balance of my air in a decompression stop. But I had an uneasy feeling about something.

Back on the boat, I removed my backpack and empty bottle and waited for Adam. After about ten minutes, I stood on the bow and peered around but could not see him, nor any telltale patch of bubbles on the calm flat water. Another ten minutes, and I was anxious. I knew I could not snorkel to 25 metres and my air bottle was empty. I radioed the volunteer coast guard and told them where we were and that I was worried. Deep down, however, I knew it was already too late. Another voice came on the radio saying they were scuba diving close by and had air bottles on board and would race around.

The other boat took about fifteen minutes to get there. I geared up again and waited for the air bottle to arrive. I knew exactly where Adam would be. I plunged down, located the boulder, and swam to where I had last seen him. He was still there, upside down, right by the hole, slowly swaying back and forth like the kelp. No air was coming from his mouthpiece.

Sometimes you vaguely sense things may be wrong, but on this occasion, for some reason, I had a premonition, a picture in my mind as clear as a photograph. I knew what was wrong. I went closer, right to the bottom. Adam's hand was still in the hole where he had seen the crayfish. I shone my torch in beside his arm. Blood wept from both sides of his wrist, where the massive lobster still had a firm grip with its huge claws. His wrist and the claws formed a wedge that had jammed in the narrow entrance, the crayfish unable to let Adam go, and Adam unable to release his grip on the lobster.

THE PHOENIX

JOHNNY NAMED his 45-foot fishing boat Phoenix for a good reason: it represented his rebirth with a new business, a new wife and a new boat. The 2008 property crash had cost him everything. The Receiver had seized all his properties and vehicles—even his boat; his bitchy spendthrift wife had run off with his crooked accountant. The pair of them had brought him nothing but misfortune, and he left with just the clothes he was wearing.

But Johnny was an optimist and had always considered himself lucky. His business deals, devised by his accountant, were not quite illegal, so Johnny was never prosecuted, let alone jailed as his wife predicted. Eventually, his seized assets realised enough to meet his liabilities, so he could pay his debts and avoid bankruptcy. Some of his old friends shunned him, preferring to socialise with his ex-wife, but that freed Johnny to focus on starting again. Just as the mythical phoenix bird burned on a funeral pyre and rose from the ashes, so too did Johnny.

The second time around, he found it was quicker. He changed lawyers; he changed banks, and he sure as hell changed accountants. Many of the people he had dealt with before still trusted him, but it was a year before he bought his first property, and he put a lot of sweat equity into the project. It was five years before the market upturn significantly pushed up values. By then, he had four commercial properties and enjoyed charting his rapid progress back into the multi-million dollar club on a graph.

It was the same with personal relationships. Tina, his new partner, was no party girl, but she was attractive and helpful. She worked as his lawyer's receptionist, and after a couple of dates, he shifted in with her, joking that it was only to save rent. As soon as his divorce came through, Johnny married Tina, and he knew his life had changed for the better.

His new fishing boat was bigger and better than the earlier one. Some told him he was lucky, and Johnny laughed and said, 'You're dead right,' but privately, he attributed much of his newfound luck to Tina! He took particular pleasure in negotiating a heavily discounted cash purchase price with the same Receiver that had wound up his affairs a few years earlier.

Once he got possession of the boat, he was anxious to try it out, so eager that he defied the adverse weather forecast. All of his invited mates pulled out at the last moment. One pointed out that during the equinox New Zealand always has foul weather. But Johnny said, 'I'm going to celebrate getting a boat again with you or without you, come hell or high water'. His mates predicted he would get both! When he told the coastguard he wanted to fish at Astrolabe Reef, they strongly advised him against leaving Tauranga Harbour.

As he headed northeast, the sea was not too rough, about a metre and a half of swell on his bow. He experimented with the revs of the twin diesels and adjusted the trim until the Phoenix was splitting aside the sea at close to twenty knots. He looked back at the fading, shrinking Mount, its peak covered in swirling low cloud, and saw his wide foaming wake in the deepening swell. The dissipating wake was like a set of footprints in falling snow, leaving no path to follow. Johnny was sailing into the zone where a descending depression in the north would meet a high-pressure complex slowly coming up the east coast, duplicating recent cyclone conditions.

His confidence, undiminished by the falling glass because he thought he could always turn and run and be back inside the entrance in under an hour. But the mutually incompatible fronts were reducing the swell in front of him but raising it in his wake. It was as if gentle fingers were encircling him, drawing him out, wooing him towards its deadly centre.

The enclosing clouds darkened the day as if he was within a low black dome the size of a sports stadium. As he approached Astrolabe, the swells riding up the sloping ocean floor of the reef exploded upwards, sending white spray 30 metres in the air. He throttled back and veered away to face Motiti Island. The first passing swell lifted him high, and his boat spun 180 degrees around on the white-crested cap to meet the next looming swell that rose like a wall before him, exposing the jagged rocks of Astrolabe.

His thoughts were now of surviving, avoiding being smashed upon the rocks or swamped by the crashing waves. He thrust the linked throttles forward and spun the wheel but, before the Phoenix answered his desperate call, the swell smashed into the reef and piled a half-metre layer of broken water across the bow. The weight of water made her pause, like an Olympic weight-lifter, before he wrenches the bar upwards. The boat broke free with a roar of jubilation. Johnny ran before the swell, not towards home, but away from Astrolabe and death, towards the now invisible Motiti Island.

As he regained control of her speed and direction, he matched the boat speed to that of the following swell, knowing that any single wave breaking over the stern could swamp her. After the boat broke free of the ambit of Astrolabe, she struck the raging complex cross-chops coming from both north and east. Johnny had to drop his revs back and handle the sea on a second-to-second basis, turning and accelerating to face a breaking swell from the east and then slowing, but not too much, to ride out a crashing wave behind. His efforts became a losing battle because the bilge pumps could no longer handle the water she was taking on, and with the extra weight, she gradually became too sluggish to respond. One rogue wave misjudged, and the Phoenix would founder, to become a wreck upon the ocean floor 10 or 12 nautical miles from the Papamoa coast.

But the end for the Phoenix came by different means,

driven against a submerged boulder near the Hole-in-the-Rock at the north end of Motiti, ripping her hull open, flooding the engine compartment. But still, she would not sink because as she lay over, drifting in the driving sea towards Plate Island, the gash faced upwards. She was stable, if not mobile, and Johnny clung first to the dead helm, wet and bruised but surviving, as she was driven further southeast by the northerly depression. The course of nature's battle between two weather systems mattered little as he squeezed into the cabin, out of the screaming wind and driving rain.

They searched for nearly a week and, perversely, found a few bits and pieces from the Phoenix, in the opposite direction, near Mayor Island. They found two life jackets in Crater Bay, and the big deck ice-Eski washed into South-East Bay. A plane flew as far north as the Aldermens, but they could not find Phoenix or Johnny's body. That was understandable because the Phoenix had smashed into Plate Island 50 kilometres away and gone down there in 30 metres of water. Her deck Eski, life jackets and other floating debris had been blown north to Mayor when the eastern high-pressure zone overcame the northern depression.

Johnny, never a good swimmer, had kicked the short distance to Plate Island, using a small chilli-bin for flotation, and had clambered up the steep rocky shoreline, dragging the bin with him. After the first couple of days, the curious seals ignored him in his nest of scrub and bracken, and he waited for the storm to abate. On the tenth day, he awoke to the sound of divers donning wet suits and scuba equipment on their boat 10 metres below his nest.

The divers were amazed to see the apparition arise above them among the ash-coloured rocks. They threw Johnny a line and dragged him and his Eski across the water to their boat. After establishing he was the missing fisherman, one diver asked, 'Do you know how long you have been missing?

'Sure! Ten days,' replied Johnny.

'What did you survive on?' a second diver asked, looking at the flushed, healthy-looking Johnny.

'I was pretty lucky. Each day I rationed myself to two corned beef sandwiches, a piece of bacon and egg pie, and a stubbie! Tina packed lunch for four of us, and I chucked in a dozen of stubbies of beer. Today though, I'll give the sandwiches a miss, they've gone a bit mouldy, but I might drink my last two beers and borrow a cell phone off you guys so I can ring Tina while you fellas go diving.'

A SEDENTARY OCCUPATION

AS HAROLD THREW the anchor over, my buddy asked, 'where did you meet this fellow? and what does he do for a living?'

'He has just transferred down from head office in Auckland in the same company that I work for, employed as a consultant of some sort,' I replied.

'A sedentary occupation,' my mate said sceptically. 'Can't you just tell?'

I hadn't thought about it before, but it was pretty obvious: Harold was overweight, his complexion was all pink with white blotches, and it didn't help that his hair had receded, giving him a Friar Tuck look.

'He looks like a big blubbery seal, but we'll soon see what he's like in the water,' said my buddy.

We geared up: my buddy with his one-metre fins; me with my powerful split fins; and Harold with an old pair of faded blue fins. He had an old metallic gun that looked pretty worn with a single rubber, but his spear seemed freshly sharpened. Instead of a plastic float, he had a piece of net laced into an inner tube held by a piece of clothesline rope threaded around his weight belt. He tied a couple of half hitches to keep it there, and we all jumped in the water.

Harold said he would stay close to where we had anchored and keep an eye on the boat. He flopped into the water, like a walrus, paddling slowly in a circle, looking at the enormous rocks, some covered in kelp, others bald and white, hosting colonies of kina. My buddy rolled his eyes in wonder at this action and said he was going over to the whitewater on the point to see what traffic was passing by. He armed up his double-rubber French speargun, and with slow, rhythmic strokes of his long fins, he was soon well away. I was going in the opposite direction to crunch up several patches of kina in the murky, deep water under the face of the cliff to try and bring out some decent-sized snapper. So I powered off in that direction.

We usually snorkel for an hour or so and then meet back

at the boat to have a snack and a hot drink and chat about what we had caught or seen; if there were few fish about, we would shift the boat to try for better luck somewhere else. By the time I had carefully selected three suitable places, smashed kina up, and gone paddling off to allow the fish to be attracted, nearly an hour had passed. In a deep fissure about ten metres down, I saw a few crayfish, catching one small but legal male and securing him in one of the nylon loops hanging from my fish float. At the first call around the traps, there was only a moray eel and a few parrotfish; at the second location, there were some leather jackets, a couple of angelfish scrapping with each other over territory and two small snapper that bolted as I got close. As I drifted slowly down upon the third patch, there was a nice-sized snapper, head down, gutsing on the kina, and I got him with a body shot. I knew I would have to trim around where the fillets would have holes stained with blood. It struggled as I grabbed it, but eventually, I got my fish spike in one gill and out through its mouth, freed my spear, and reloaded my gun.

My buddy swam up and down beyond the point, eventually seeing some kingfish come towards him out of curiosity, but they never ventured close enough for him to get a shot away. As we returned, we met up, and without saying anything, we both wondered how Harold was getting on. We swam in across the current towards the stern end of the boat. As we passed his inner tube, we saw the net beneath was full of fish. Among about a dozen brilliant-blue maomao were a big snapper, a couple of greenbone, two kahawai, and a medium-sized kingfish. As far as we could tell, all showed the sign of perfect headshots.

The visibility under the boat was reasonably good. As we approached, we could vaguely see Harold about 12 metres below with his back to us, sitting in the shade behind a fold of a bare rock, surrounded by a frenzy of fish. They were feeding on the drift of smashed up kina. There were hundreds of iridescent blue maomao, a selection of odds and sods inter-mingled with them, and further out was a school of circling kahawai. As we looked down again, closer now, we could see Harold had his spear gun pointing out from his hiding place, like a duck shooter waiting patiently in a mai mai on a riverbank. A john dory was approaching the activity around the rock, and the aim of the shiny point of Harold's spear shifted imperceptibly and then unleashed to penetrate the hapless fish with another good headshot. As Harold slowly drifted upwards, he was simultaneously pulling in the fish with one hand and his inner tube with the other. As he met up with his net on the surface, he already had his gloved hand over the john dory and expertly flicked it into the net.

Only then did he see us, smiling and waving his greetings, and we all climbed back on board. My buddy was exhausted from his long swim; I was feeling the effect of my deep repetition dives, while Harold seemed as fresh as a daisy. As we munched on our bread rolls, I asked him what particular job he did in the office.

'Nothing important: I'm a time and motion consultant,' he replied.

DIFFERENT STROKES

AFTER GETTING BACK from the club dive trip, Smithy and Mark, who had only met that morning, were in a group having a beer at the Mount Ocean Sports Club. They had both dived on scuba that day, but Smithy had gone freediving with a speargun around Plate Island while the others watched and ate their lunch. Mark, a real estate agent, was 25, tall and a little paunchy. His casual clothes were as immaculate as his carefully groomed hair.

'I watched you swim,' he said to Smithy. 'You looked pretty good. Were you ever a competitive swimmer?'

Smithy was shorter, younger, maybe 22, tanned, hard-muscled, and his fair hair bleached from working as a carpenter, 'Only when I was at school. Then I had to get out and earn a living.'

'Where were you from originally?' asked the agent.

'Feilding. I came up here for the work,' replied Smithy.

'How good were you?' asked Mark.

'At swimming? Pretty good! But it's all relative, isn't it?'

The others in the group watched, becoming a little more interested in this tentative exchange that was beginning to seem like a couple of stags facing off after an accidental encounter in the bush.

'I was pretty good myself,' said Mark, 'But I was in a swim squad with a professional coach in Auckland. As you say, it's all relative.'

It wasn't the words that upset Smithy but the condescending tone. He overreacted: 'Yeah! But you would be well past it now!' It came out worse than he had intended. It was his first club dive, and he hadn't joined the Underwater Club to have silly scraps.

He finished his beer, intending to leave, but the real estate agent was not happy. 'I could show you a clean pair of heels any day.'

'Maybe … maybe not,' said Smithy. He intended his words to appease Mark, but his tone was critical and dismissive and mistakenly interpreted as a challenge.

'Well, you might have to put your money where your mouth is,' said Mark.

Smithy smiled and said, 'Difficult to prove one way or the other, though, isn't it?'

Instead of leaving, Smithy went to get another beer. Another diver from the leaner joined him at the bar. He said quietly to Smithy, 'Mark was a New Zealand champ a few years ago.' Smithy's face was blank, almost non-committal, perhaps just slightly bemused.

'He was the National 4 by 100 Medley champion,' added the other. 'Nearly got to the Olympics. Damn good swimmer even now.'

Smithy smiled, 'So what?'

'So you'd be wasting your money, that's what!'

'Only if I lost!'

The other man looked at him, shrugging at Smithy's stubbornness and lack of gratitude for their advice. 'Please yourself,' he said.

They walked back to the leaner, and before they had set their handles down, Mark asked, 'You on, or what?'

'What did you have in mind?' asked Smithy.

'A pool swim,' said Mark confidently.

'When and where?' said Smithy.

'At Baywave at five on Friday night.'

'How much?' asked Smithy.

'Fifty bucks,' suggested Mark.

'Make it a hundred!' said Smithy. 'There's a condition, though.' The other divers at the leaner leaned forward, totally intrigued.

'What's that?' asked Mark with mock curiosity.

'I choose the stroke and distance.'

'Okay! So what's your stroke and distance?'

'Well, dunno, 50 or 100 metres, I think. Maybe 200 metres!' said Smithy. 'But I won't nominate the stroke or distance until Friday.'

The group from the leaner and a few others gathered at the pool at the allotted time. The pool lanes were in place, and a couple of kids were playing about on one side of the pool, while an old grey-haired guy was ploughing back and forth on the other side, doing his twice-weekly workout.

Mark and Smithy got changed and were ready to start.

'So what's the stroke?' the taller man asked calmly.

'I thought backstroke, and 200 metres?' said Smithy as if he did not care.

'Fine! It doesn't matter one way or the other to me. Did you know I was a New Zealand Medley Champion six years ago?'

'Yeah, sure! I watched you win that title. I was in the same final two years later, when the winner broke your record. I led for the butterfly and backstroke legs and should have won the damn thing, but I am no bloody good at breaststroke.'

Mark went very quiet.

'I imagine you'll be in front for the first 50 metres,' said Smithy. 'After 100 metres, I'll probably be close alongside. After 150, who knows, but as we finish, I think you may be regretting your bet!'

CATCH OF THE DAY

DOLL FINN HAD ALWAYS BEEN a bit of a tom-boy, despite her good looks and spectacular figure. It was unusual that a shapely young woman had always liked playing with boys. But when boys tried playing with her, she brought into full effect her Australian vocabulary. She was the only child of an outback pub-owner, and as a schoolgirl, had regularly gone hunting with her father and his mates, learning how to shoot wild game and skin a kangaroo. So she was used to handling stroppy men and was not shy when she gravitated into situations where she was the only woman in men's company.

After a bit of tramping and scuba diving around New Zealand, she tried phoning to book a place on a charter boat called Fat Boy and discovered the skipper still had space on a fishing trip the next day. The skipper warned her that two men had taken the other places and that he would check that they didn't mind.

'Didn't mind what?' asked Doll.

'Didn't mind an outsider going with them—they're great mates and know each other well,' he diplomatically replied.

When he rang back and said it was okay by the others, she asked what she needed to bring.

'Just yourself and some lunch,' he replied, 'And no bananas!'

'What are ya?' she replied, a little sarcastically.

They arranged to meet at 6 am the following day at the Pilot Bay launching ramp, and when Doll arrived, the men already had the boat in the water and watched her walk up. One of them, a tall slim young fellow, made a low whistle she could not hear, and the other two just stared.

She walked straight past the skipper up to one of the fishermen, a giant of a man with a considerable waistline, and stuck out her hand and said, 'I'm Doll Finn, you must be Fat Boy.'

He looked her up and down as they shook hands, 'I'm

Slim Jim. I didn't mention your gorgeous figure, so how come you mentioned mine?'

Doll was a bit perplexed until the skipper intervened, 'I'm the skipper, not him, and it's the boat that's called Fat Boy.'

'While we are on the subject, I'm Gutsy Guthrie,' said the tall thin man who had whistled as she arrived. Doll rolled her eyes at this but did not comment.

They offered to pull the boat closer in for her, but she pulled her sneakers off, rolled her jeans up, waded out just like them, and clambered up the ladder. As they left the entrance, the skipper radioed the coastguard that they were heading out past Astrolabe for puka.

'What are puka?' asked Doll.

'It's short for hapuku,' replied Slim.

'But we don't usually catch hapuku, we usually catch bluenose,' said Gutsy.

'I catch a blue nose when I'm tramping, especially at high altitude,' said Doll Finn, smiling, but failing to get a laugh, except the skipper.

'Bluenose is a fish a bit like hapuku,' he said

'Now let's get this straight: Slim is fat; Gutsy is skinny: Fat Boy is a boat. We are fishing for puka, but we are really after bluenose. Why don't you kiwis speak plain bloody English instead of confusing people all the time?' she said.

Slim and Gutsy stared at each other in disbelief.

When they arrived at the secret spot, Slim and Gutsy rigged their rods while the skipper fixed up a rod for himself and another for Doll. The boat bobbed around in half a metre or so of swell, and he pulled gimbals and harnesses from forward.

He showed these bits of equipment to Doll Finn, who said, 'What the hell do I do with these?'

'Puka can get pretty big,' said the skipper, 'and the gimbal holds the rod and the harness is clipped to the reel, so you don't lose your gear overboard.'

'They look to me as if they came in a plain brown wrapper and you use them at funny parties.'

This time the others did laugh.

'I'll help you into them,' said Russ.

'And I'll help you out of them,' said Gutsy, eyeing his fishing companion.

'You can both keep your hands to your-bloody-selves,' she said, taking the gimbal from the skipper and following his instructions on donning it.

'Sometimes we have a pool, so much in for the biggest fish, a catch of the day prize,' said Slim as he baited up with long strips of bonito.

'Okay,' said Doll Finn, 'I'm a player.'

The two men looked at each other and smiled slyly. The skipper wondered if their grinning resulted from the double meaning of her words or the prospect of a bet.

'How much?' asked Gutsy.

'The price of the day out,' said Doll without hesitating.

'You're on,' they said in unison.

'Biggest fish landed without any help,' said the skipper.

They dropped their lines simultaneously, the heavy weights unravelling the reels quickly down to more than two hundred metres. They lifted their weighted lines just off the floor and waited while the boat bobbed and floated on the open sea. Slim got the first strike, and he worked his rod up with his vast bulk, reeling in as he lowered the rod, settling into a steady rhythm.

'It's a long way up from 200 metres,' said the skipper to Doll.

'You just take it steady,' said Gutsy helpfully.

'If you realised what a dick you look, you wouldn't do that,' said Doll Finn to Slim.

'At least it's a familiar feeling,' he retorted. 'We'll see what you look like if you get so lucky.'

Just as Slim's fish appeared, and as the skipper passed him the gaff, Doll Finn and Gutsy Guthrie got simultaneous strikes and began the task of hauling their fish up from the depths.

'12.5 kilos to beat!' said Slim as he held his fish on the small electronic scales.

'Bugger!' said Doll, nursing her slack line, 'I've lost mine!'

Gutsy kept reeling away, and when he saw the colour of the fish, he took the gaff and jagged it firmly into the fish.

As he hauled it on board, a second fish appeared out of the gloom, 'I've got two,' Gutsy said and gaffed the second and dragged it up, together with Doll's weight and hooks tangled around his line.

'Hey, that's my fish,' she said. 'It's on my line, and it's the biggest by far.'

'Tough!' said Gutsy. 'I landed it ... and all by myself ... and them's the rules!'

They re-baited their lines and, after shifting the boat back over the exact spot, they dropped their lines back down. Doll Finn became very sullen. Her father had told her not to whine but never to take crap from men. She thought of saying something about underarm bowling being sometimes justified, but she bit her tongue.

If we don't get another bite soon, we might shift on and see if there are some tarakihi in closer to Motiti,' said the skipper.

Doll, knowing tarakihi was a smaller fish than bluenose, bit her tongue even harder.

Gutsy's line tautened, and his rod bent over: 'Wowee!' he

said and started reeling. His long skinny frame made hard work of the big fish, and he rested from time to time as he worked the fish upwards. When they first sighted it, they knew it was the winning fish. Gutsy had one final rest as the boat swung slightly in the current. When he began reeling again, the line had wrapped around the stern of the boat, and his reeling caused the fish to wrench free. It drifted off behind them, still floating because its airbags had inflated, and it was moving away from the boat.

Skip said, 'Reel in the other lines, and I'll back up so you can gaff it.'

But Doll shoved her rod in the holder, stripped off her gimbal and harness, then her shirt and jersey in one go, then her sneakers and jeans. She grabbed the gaff and leapt over the back into the sea in her knickers and bra. She gaffed the fish in one vicious swipe and towed it back to the boat.

'Don't touch it!' she shouted and slung it on the transom as if she was throwing a calf down for branding. She climbed up the ladder with water pouring off her near-naked body and the men gawking like teenage boys.

'Whose bloody fish is this one then!' she asked.

DE NADA

CLEM FOSS and I were at a leaner having a beer as the Whitianga pub gradually filled up. Clem was younger than me, still in his early twenties. Eventually, all the leaners were more or less fully occupied, and a couple of guys came up and gestured to the other end of our leaner.

I shrugged, and Foss said, 'De nada!'

The big fat guy, red-faced and flustered even before he had a drink, said, 'What!' It was more an exclamation than a question.

'It means 'She'll be right in Spanish,' I said, being familiar with Foss's recent use of the expression, although I never knew where or how he had picked it up. All I knew was that he had recently returned from his big OE and seemed a lot quieter after nearly two years away.

'Is your mate a dago or something?' asked the taller of the two men. He had parallel creases running down at an angle from his eyes, nose and mouth, giving him a permanently sad, almost sour, look.

'No, I'm a kiwi,' said Foss, 'and to say de nada is to accept your fate without casting blame.'

The men just grunted, and each took a long sip on his beer. 'What I don't like about this place is the bloody lousy service,' said the shorter man with a flushed face.

They weren't talking directly to us, but it was apparent they didn't mind our hearing. 'You just struck a busy patch,' I said calmly and wondered what their hurry was.

'It wouldn't be so bad if that bird behind the bar wasn't so ugly,' said the taller one.

There was no suitable answer to that comment, so I remained silent, but I wondered to myself whether they had come to the clubrooms for a beer or some sort of fantasy sexual experience. Looking at them, I concluded that they were hardly God's gift to women themselves.

'They should do something about it,' said the shorter one.

'Should sack her,' said the taller.

Someone carrying four handles of beer, two in each hand, pushed past us and slopped beer on Clem; a small amount dribbled down his shirt and trousers and onto his shoes.

'Sorry, mate,' the intruder said.

'De nada,' said Foss.

'What are ya?' said Redface, 'I would've whacked him.'

'Worse things have happened to me,' said Foss.

'Yeah, sure! De nada!' said Redface sarcastically.

'Talking about worse things,' said the tall man, scowling. 'I lost my outboard overboard yesterday. I was lifting it back onto the transom when the wake of a passing boat made me slip, and I had to let it go. Two-bloody-thousand bucks worth. No insurance because the safety chain wasn't on. How the hell could I put the safety chain on until I had the motor in position?'

'De nada,' said Redface, looking aggressively at Foss. Foss and I looked at each other without speaking. I wondered where all this was leading.

'Bloody insurance companies,' said Redface. 'A couple of months ago the wheel studs on my four-wheel-drive came loose, and when they wrenched free, the whole friggin' wheel assembly collapsed, wrecking the rim, ripping open the $200 tyre, and then, as I skidded to a stop, my boat jack-knifed against a Mercedes. More than $5000 worth of damage.'

'They'd have to pay out on that, though,' said his companion.

'They said they would at first. Then the insurer sent an assessor to the repair shop. He said one tyre was bald, and it blew out, causing all the damage. So now they say it was my fault.'

'Bloody wrong isn't,' agreed his mate.

Foss and I did not say a word I swear it. But I must admit that I damn nearly said, 'De nada!'

Sadsack did not notice, but Redface glared at Fossie as if he had felt the de nada vibrations coming from him. 'I suppose worse things have happened to you?' he said to Fossie, blaming the wrong man.

'Yes,' replied Foss, who seemed to be getting a little agitated.

'You better tell us about it then,' said Sadsack, joining in the provocation.

'Rather not,' said Foss abruptly.

'Come on,' said Redface. 'We shared our hard-luck stories with you; now it's your turn.'

'I said I'd rather not,' Foss repeated, and after pausing, he added angrily, 'Your stupidity can hardly be called bad luck. Who gives a fuck about your boats and cars? What does insurance do: replace wheels, motors, fix a bit of panel work?'

Redface looked at Sadsack and laughed: 'Some story! De nada!'

Foss ignored them; he ignored me too, for that matter. He was looking down, trying to keep control of himself. His grip on his handle was so fierce the surface of the beer quivered. After a minute or so, the beer was still, he had calmed, and he started, slowly and quietly: 'A few months back, I went to a Flamenco nightclub in Madrid. Teresa wasn't the star dancer, just a young student. When our eyes met, it was one of those things that you only ever read about or see in the movies. I had a camera with a flash, and every time I tried to take her photo, the star dancer would pose in front of Teresa. Eventually, the male lead dancer whispered something to the older dancer, and she gestured for Teresa to take the lead role with the male dancer. I got some nice photos. It was a strange experience as if she was dancing just for me.'

He removed his wallet and pulled a well-worn photo from behind his banknotes, and looked at it. Redface reached out to look at it, but Foss quickly returned the photograph to his wallet.

The noise in the pub had picked up as the crowd increased, but the two men at our leaner were deathly silent, listening intently. Fossie continued: 'I tried to go backstage after the show, but the steward stopped me: 'No visitar!' he said. But Teresa had changed very quickly and came out to see if I was still there. She smiled and said she could only speak a little English and would meet me across the road for coffee, but could do so only briefly, and that I should wait for her at the café while she explained to her instructor, Senora Carmen, where she was going.'

Foss's face had gone grey; his eyes focussed far away: 'It was a cold, wet night, and I had rubbed a patch clear on the steamed-up window of the café so I could see Teresa coming. I wish now I had waited outside in the rain for her. The door of the club opened just as the car screeched around the corner. I never actually saw it happen because I was halfway to the door to try and stop her. I heard the thump, though and raced out into the rain. I dropped to my knees beside her. She smiled up at me and softly whispered, 'De nada,' and then she died.'

KOTUKU

Note for the reader: this story was written before Donald Trump was ever mentioned as a presidential candidate for the Republican Party.

'WHO THE HELL ARE YOU? Get out of the elevator!' The dark-suited guy was hauling out a 38 Smith and Wesson and pointing it at my chest.

'I'm Secret Service!' he added as if that would justify blowing me away.

'My name is Joe,' I said, my eyes scanning the faces at the

lift door and the crowded foyer behind them. 'Goin' up?' I asked, smiling, even though I was shit-scared.

'Get out! Don't you know who these people are?' The suit was waving his gun.

'No, can't say I do—but I don't mind sharing the lift with them.' My eyes met those of a woman with a diamond-encrusted crucifix on a gold chain around her neck. She had looked bored but was smiling now as I defied the bodyguard.

'I will get out—on level seventeen,' I said.

The next ten seconds seemed longer, more like ten minutes.

Ignoring the gun, the blonde sauntered into the lift and stopped, facing me, one hand on her hip, one thumb stuck in the air. She raised one eyebrow. 'Hi, Joe. I'm Carolyn. Thanks for the lift.' Then she glanced back over her shoulder, 'Good work, Turnbull. It's not midday yet, and you're dying to have a shootout.'

She lingered on the word 'dying', the same as Georgie Fame does with 'pool of blood' in *The Ballad of Bonnie and Clyde*.

'So kill this Muslim terrorist if you must, but you clean up the mess,' she said.

Carolyn was straight out of *The Big Sleep*—the blonde who draped herself across the PI's desk. I was Humphrey Bogart.

An African-American, short and slightly overweight, had slipped into the lift beside her. The front left of his jacket bulged, but he seemed relieved at his charge's action and pissed off with the other bodyguard. 'Come on, Turnbull. This guy's harmless.' He rolled his eyes at me.

Turnbull entered the lift, scowling as he reholstered his gun. He was followed by the local Republican Party chairman and his wife, both in their mid-sixties, both visibly shaken after sighting the gun. They waited as another man, with steel-grey hair and matching suit, both military-cut, took documents from a group in the middle of the foyer, folded them vertically and slipped them into the inside pocket of his jacket.

The senator brushed non-existent dust from his sleeve and entered the elevator. 'Tell me more about the guy doing the intro—something personal. Married? Children? What's he do? What's his angle? Is he properly briefed?' He began noting the chairman's responses.

Carolyn was still facing me, close enough for me to notice her delicate perfume and feel the radiating warmth of her skin. Her closeness was nice—a little unnerving, but nice—and she still held my gaze.

'Thanks, Carolyn. Being executed was not on my plan.' I looked at her trim cream skirt and matching jacket, only briefly losing eye contact. 'Loved your timing, but you're not really dressed for the role.'

'Right, Joe, but like you, sometimes I improvise.' Her green eyes scanned my face.

The elevator had risen to level five. It stopped smoothly, the doors opened, and a sweet recorded voice said: 'Level five—the ballroom.' The senator, who had finished making notes, strode out of the lift, followed by Turnbull, the party people and Carolyn's black bodyguard. My right arm snaked forward and gripped Carolyn's forearm. I felt her go tense, then relax, as her eyes challenged me. Only the black bodyguard was still close to the elevator. He stepped back between the closing doors, only just making it, and his hand slid into his jacket. Over Carolyn's shoulder, I could see his eyes begging me to let her go.

'I'm all right, Wes,' she said, still smiling but demanding I answer.

'Why don't you come out sailing with me this afternoon?' I said.

Astonished, Carolyn tossed her head back and laughed.

Shaking his head in disbelief, Wes took Carolyn by one arm as I reluctantly released the other. I stopped the lift door and watched her walk away. She looked back, just once, and then caught up to her Republican husband, who was expecting to be elected president of the United States in three days.

The elevator rose to level seventeen. I felt stunned as if a whole day had passed in a few minutes. God, I must be mad. But it was real—Carolyn was undoubtedly real—and so was that gun! I walked into the law firm's foyer, trying to refocus.

The receptionist looked up and smiled. 'Mr Cassell is expecting you. We all had to show our IDs this morning.' How did you manage with the security down below?

'I'm still shell-shocked,' I replied.

In Cassell's office, the lawyer laid out the documents: the title to the yacht and the security release; the authority to leave US waters; my stamped passport, a customs declaration and the lawyer's supporting affidavit. 'And last, our account,' the lawyer said. 'I believe my secretary has discussed the final payment with you?'

'Yes, I have a bank cheque.' I placed the envelope on the desk.

'So when do you leave for Auckland, Joe?'

'Friday at the earliest; Sunday at the latest. I only have provisions to stow. When I've done that, I'll lift *Kotuku* into the water.'

'What does *Kotuku* mean, Joe?'

'It's the Māori name for our lovely white heron,' I replied. 'Tell me, is Senator Cranston really going to be president?'

'Oh! You saw the show downstairs? Madonna was the last

one to cause such chaos. Well, Cranston has never led in electoral votes. Pundits say he cannot win, but he should never be written off. In the senate race eight years ago, he was well behind in the polls, and a few days before the election, extremists attempted to assassinate him. He won comfortably.'

'How can he be so popular when he appears so cold and hard?'

'War hero, Joe. We love them. Since Eisenhower, it has been that way for me, but it dates back to our first president, George Washington.'

'Strange system that elects a president on military credentials,' I commented.

'Indeed, and this election run-up has been extraordinary. The Republicans are even more doctrinaire than in 2012, totally dominated by the Tea Party, and Cranston has pandered to them on every issue. However, that strength within the party is now his weakness nationally.'

I nodded. 'Carolyn's not his first wife, is she?'

'No! His first wife died in the attempt on his life. The booby-trapped car was meant to kill Cranston. Instead, she died, and so did the driver, but that's all water under the bridge now. The word was that Carolyn Hillier would never have married him if there was anything to the silly rumours. Carolyn's father is worth more than Donald Trump, except Hillier doesn't display his wealth.'

The lawyer stood up to terminate our discussion and reached out to shake my hand.

'I took the elevator from the basement car park and came from the foyer to the ballroom level with them,' I said as we shook hands. The lawyer raised his eyebrows.

'She joked with me while we waited for the senator—I thought she was charming—and stunningly beautiful!'

'You were privileged,' said Cassell. 'No one gets to speak to *The Lady*, as she has become known. She refuses to give interviews, but Cranston has turned it to his advantage, adding a special mystique—a touch of Jackie Kennedy, if you like. It softens the hardness that you recognised. Well, good luck, Joe, and take care out there.'

The provedor's van arrived mid-afternoon, pulling up alongside *Kotuku*, resting in her steel cradle on the asphalt at the boatyard. There were about 40 cartons: frozen goods, dry goods, canned food, fresh fruit and vegetables, beer, rum and wine.

'I'll give you a hand?' offered the bearded sailor from the yacht immediately behind mine.

'Thanks, Arnie. Much appreciated.' Arnie reminded me of Sinbad the Sailor in a kid's picture book I used to have: short, bandy-legged, and usually either laughing or cursing.

The driver passed the cartons up to Arnie, who passed them down to me. I packed everything tightly to avoid any movement in rough weather.

'Hot work, Arnie,' I said as we finished. 'Feel like a cold beer?'

After we climbed down, Arnie called to his wife. 'Goin' for a beer, honey.'

Jan replied from below: 'Don't do anything I wouldn't, or I'll burn your steak—and your yacht!'

The tavern had seen better days. The bar had teak panelling and was aged and overdue for reoiling. Mounted on the walls were brass portholes green with verdigris and game fish with faded details scripted below them. The customers were fishermen and sailors, who used the bar as a clubhouse, and a group of tradesmen who lived nearby and used it as their local pub. It was the sort of place where Norman Mailer would have made a nuisance of himself after drinking too much. I bought a couple of beers, and we sat on stools at a leaner near the expansive windows facing the hardstand, where almost a hundred yachts were up out of the water for storage or maintenance. *Kotuku* and Arnie's boat were among the closest.

In the rear corner, a woman wearing tight red trousers and an even tighter top laughed at some comment made by her minder to a group of swaggering Latinos. Arnie and I sipped on our beer. The sun was low in the western sky, casting lengthening shadows from boat masts and aerials.

'So you leave in a couple of days?'

'Yep, probably Friday, on the full tide. I'll lift her into the water late tomorrow.'

I stood up and walked to the window. 'Jesus Christ!'

'What's up?' asked Arnie, following the line of my gaze.

'That woman … I know her. I met her this morning in town.'

'She'll get a rough reception if she comes in here dressed like that.'

'She may be looking for me,' I said.

The largest of the Mexicans, wearing shades and a broad moustache, had noticed her too and growled a comment to his companions. Sue, the resident hooker, was bristling.

Carolyn was wearing tight jeans and a sweater, with a dark wig covering her blonde hair. She walked twice around *Kotuku*, pausing at the steps beside my yacht, and called out. Arnie's wife, on the adjacent boat, appeared from below. After a brief conversation, Jan pointed to the bar, and Carolyn turned and flounced the short distance towards the bar steps.

'Holy shit, Joe! There's gonna be trouble now.'

'Calm down, Arnie. This lady's no hooker!'

I hurried towards the door and took Carolyn's arm as she entered.

'Carolyn cut the pose—please—Or you'll put yourself at risk from the real thing and her minders.' I led her over to the leaner and said, 'This is Arnie. Arnie, this is ...'

'Suzie!' interrupted Carolyn.

'Call yourself anything you like, baby, but not Suzie, not in here, or we're all dead meat!' said Arnie grimly.

'This is my friend—Karen,' I said. 'Okay?'

'Look, lady. Those guys in the corner—no, please don't look—they have shotguns mounted inside their SUVs. They sell H, they sell P, they sell wacky baccy; they pimp for Sue and a bunch of other ugly women in a bunch of other ugly pubs. I saw them bottle a guy in here one night just for staring at them. If they come over, don't say a word. Just leave it to me. Please!'

The construction workers near us felt the icy atmosphere spread through the bar like a drift of unseasonable snow. One was watching Carolyn, but the rest were watching the Mexican, who swaggered over towards us. He stopped, his leather jerkin was open, and a knife appeared in his hand; it flicked open to show a glinting razor-sharp edge. It was closer than an arm's length from my gut. He palmed it shut, and it vanished.

He swivelled and spoke directly to Carolyn: 'On this patch, you work for me. *Comprende, muher?*'

'Si si, el senor, pero no trabajo ahi," answered Carolyn.

'She is a friend of Joe,' said Arnie.

'That's right,' I said. 'She's no working girl. She dresses like that to fool her husband.' I winked at the Mexican, who looked Carolyn up and down, rubbing his bristly jaw as if he was Anthony Quinn in *Viva Zapata!* inspecting a horse, and I was Clint Eastwood refusing his *Fistful of Dollars*.

'Muy bonito, la senora. Muy bonito. Eef you change your mind about workin', just ask for 'ermie. Okay?'

Carolyn nodded. 'Thanks, but no thanks.'

Hermie laughed and swaggered back to his group, saying something at which his companions bellowed with laughter, and the bar returned to normal.

'Don't you usually offer your lady friends a drink, Joe?' asked Carolyn.

'Come back to *Kotuku,* and we'll have a glass of wine,' I replied.

'Better idea,' added Arnie. 'I'm outa here too.'

We went back to our boats. I helped Carolyn up the makeshift steps onto the yacht and down into the small saloon. I poured two glasses of white wine from an open bottle in the fridge.

'You're a dangerous lady, Carolyn. I've now had a gun, and a knife pulled on me.'

'You ain't seen nothin' yet, cowboy,' she laughed.

'Well, here's lookin' at ya, kid—and living through the night to talk about it!' We clinked glasses.

'To Paris,' she said, and we both smiled.

'How did you find me?' I asked.

'Easy! I went to the seventeenth floor and asked your lawyer.'

I nodded. 'I watched your husband's speech on a TV in a shop window down the street. He's one tough hombre.' I sipped a little wine. 'I watched you as well. You looked beautiful, but a little switched off the politics.'

'Thank you. I'm not so beautiful. And you are wrong about politics; I majored in political science. Being involved, however, spoils it as a spectator sport. And, frankly, the senator's politics switch me off.'

'You could always vote for Hillary Clinton,' I laughed.

'Why are you laughing? I'm a liberal, eastern-college girl. It's my father, who is a Republican. As much as I love him—my father, that is—he got me into this mess. Of course, I will vote for Hillary and the Democrats.'

I raised my eyebrows.

'I hoped I could make changes, but I was kidding myself.'

Carolyn looked across the table at me. 'You got me here under false pretences, Joe. This yacht can't sail while it is up on the asphalt.'

'I was lying. I didn't dream you would actually come. My lawyer told me you keep yourself very private—don't even do interviews.'

'No one in the campaign has wanted me to do interviews, not after I started telling the truth.'

'The truth?'

'That I believe in tolerance—that men and women are born equal—that there are some good Muslims just as there are some bad Christians—that opportunity should be fostered across all of society, not just among the privileged few.'

'If your father is a Republican, what's he think of your views?'

'He agrees with me completely. He wasn't born rich; he made his own way as a constructor, building skyscrapers. He still rides the last beam up to top off his projects.'

'And your mother?'

'She's gone now; has been for nearly ten years.'

'You don't mind me asking questions, do you?'

'No, but this conversation is all one-way traffic.'

'One more question?' I asked.

Carolyn smiled tolerantly.

'How come you married the senator, and why was it your father's fault?'

'That's two questions. I blamed my father earlier, but that

was unfair. He only introduced us, and I went out with Cranston a few times. He wined me and dined me. He can be very charming when he wants something. The pundits immediately took it up as a marriage made in political heaven: east coast money and west coast military; a Roman Catholic to balance his Protestant background—a dream team. Cranston calls it a mandate to rule the world.'

'Hell! High stakes. To me, it looks more like *Beauty and the Beast*.'

'Mmm, maybe. But there's no sign yet of Cranston turning into a noble prince. Some of it makes me sick. Turnbull and the senator's inner circle wanted me to become pregnant early in the year, timing the birth to be about now, in the campaign's last week. They ranked that ahead of their other strategies, including law and order, bashing Muslims and unions—all the same, old stuff. I refused outright. Now internal Republican polling shows the election has slipped away. They partly blame me for that. Right at the turning point of the polls, one news clip showed me laughing during one of the senator's speeches, just as he was attacking Clinton and Obama. But he can never win anyway because he's too right-wing. Even though they will not involve me, they are quite worried about what I might do next.'

'So you thought dressing up as a hooker and visiting a kiwi yachtie was a good idea?'

'I thought I would go sailing, to calm my nerves, to get through the next few days. You were right when you said I had disguised myself, but it was to fool security, not my husband. His only concern for me is how I appear when I'm on the platform with him. This afternoon, I bought a wig, went into a clothes shop, came out dressed like this, and walked straight past Wes. I must tell his lovely wife that he was the only man I passed who did not look me up and down with salacious intent. When I was down the street, I rang him and told him I had gone to visit a friend and not to worry.'

'You didn't fool me. I recognised you from over at the bar. If you'd been wearing a burkha, I would have known it was you inside. And, frankly, it would probably have been safer.'

Carolyn flushed a little. 'I had to disguise myself somehow, or I would have been all over the news again. As it is, one of the construction workers in the bar recognised me. His yellow jacket had the big H of Hillier Construction on it. He stared at me the whole time, then used his cell phone, hopefully just calling Leftie, my father.'

'Presumably, Leftie doesn't refer to his politics?'

'No, when he was young, he was a left-handed boxer. Strangely, he is naturally right-handed, except when he was boxing.'

'You mix with tough guys. I hardly fit the pattern—a very ordinary kiwi yachtie.'

'Very ordinary indeed! You must be joking!' no reaction to guns and knives, about to sail alone across the Pacific Ocean.

'I have another question.'

Carolyn posed a pout of annoyance but with a submerged smile.

'What really happened to Cranston's first wife?'

Carolyn's smile vanished. Her face hardened, but her cell phone trilled a friendly musical call from her purse, curtailing any response. She stroked the phone. 'Father, what took you so long?'

I tried to picture the caller: James Cagney playing an Irish, whisky-drinking ex-boxer made good, protecting and spoiling his lovely daughter. Carolyn was doing all the listening. She had that Lauren Bacall bemused look again, calmly holding my gaze. I felt as if she was downloading my memories and feelings, including how much I was attracted to her.

'Yes, Father, that's right—Yes, Father, that's right—Yes, Father, we have had this conversation before—several times in fact—No, that hasn't happened—No, emphatically not!'

I sensed a warm sharing in Carolyn's eyes, a merging of our minds, a cerebral excitement that was partly intellectual, partly physical. I wondered what the questions were to receive such answers.

'The future will write itself—and I will trust and follow my own feelings—Thank you, Daddy. I love you too! Must go now—Ciao!'

Carolyn and I looked at each other with a mixture of anticipation and nervousness.

'I'm leaving now, Joe, but we will see each other again soon—very soon, I hope.'

'I hope so too. What's your cell phone number, Carolyn?' I pulled out my phone and tapped it in. I touched the call icon, and Carolyn's phone trilled again.

'Hello, Sailor!' she said in a sexy voice and clicked it off again.

Our phones had now joined our little conspiracy.

She called a cab to the gate of the marina, kissed me softly and quickly on one cheek, firmly holding me at arm's length, and skipped up the few steps to the deck. Then she made her way down the steps to ground level.

It was becoming clear that the marriage made in heaven had the fingerprints of Satan all over it, and I had never intended dealing with the Devil. I was only interested in an angel called Carolyn.

I woke early and turned on the radio. The music channel had been interrupted, and Senator Cranston was broadcasting live.

'This is terrorism, an act of war against the United States of America. Obama and the Democratic administration have always been soft on Islamic extremism. They have brought this calamity on the good people of our great nation. There must be swift retribution for those responsible for the loss of American lives.'

'Why do you believe this is an act of terrorism, Senator?' asked the interviewer.

'The explosions that preceded the collapse of the Oakland Bridge prove the president's claim that metal fatigue may have caused the bridge failure to be shallow and irresponsible. This terrorist act is a repeat of 9/11 and an act of war against the United States of America. We already know how Mrs Clinton handled the Islamist attack in Benghazi—she did nothing. It cost American lives, including our ambassador, and she has lied to our people about it ever since. Our nation needs strong and honest leadership.'

'That was presidential candidate, Senator Cranston, soon to be President Cranston. Thank you, Senator. We are now going live to the site of the tragedy.'

The radio station began interviewing witnesses at the bridge, who described the death and destruction and asked police and firefighters about searching for survivors and their desperate rescue efforts. Calls flooded into the station demanding revenge.

I flicked on the switch to make coffee and called Carolyn.

'Don't go anywhere, Joe. I'll call you later; this place is teeming with security.' The phone went dead.

I went up on deck and called out, 'Get up, Arnie before the missiles arrive.'

Arnie appeared. 'I had nightmares last night about Hermie knifing me because of you and your fancy lady. But

Jan woke me to tell me about the Oakland Bridge. Jesus, this is deadly serious.'

'Sure is, but hopefully not as deadly as the Twin Towers,' I said. 'Look, Arnie. I was going to sort my surplus gear today, and I thought you might want some of it.'

'Your paint trestle will come in handy. Some of the other stuff could be useful too.' I'm all sanded down and ready to go.

'What about the left-over hull paint? I'm not taking it with me.'

'Hey! There's enough left to paint my boat up to the waterline.'

'It's yours, Arnie. You've helped me. I owe it to you. You and Jan have been great neighbours. We could paint today. I'm not anxious to go anywhere. There'll be cops all over the place—and I've got the boat hoist coming later.'

'You're on, buddy! It's a good forecast, for now at least. Did you hear that, Jan?'

We laid out the brushes, rollers and cans of paint on an old tarp, already marked with the blue of my hull paint. Jan ran masking tape around the waterline as I brush-painted around the prop mounting and anchor entry. Arnie followed Jan with a roller, painting halfway down to the keel, and I followed with my roller, working on my knees on a thick wad of sponge rubber. When we had progressed halfway along the first side, my phone rang.

'I can come over, Joe, but Wes will be with me, on watch in the car park. The whole place has gone onto red alert. The confirmed death toll in California is up to forty-three and rising. The senator was going to hit six states today but has cancelled most, wanting to stay close to Washington.'

'Yeah, it's all over the news. We're painting Arnie's boat, so bring some old working clothes; you might want to help.'

'I don't have any *working* clothes, let alone *old* working clothes, but I'll wear something due for the charity bin. See you soon, Joe!' Her words were soft and seductive; my mixed feelings of pleasure and fear returned.

Carolyn arrived with Wes but walked over to the yacht alone. She had tied her hair up in an orange bandana; she was openly and unmistakably the Carolyn Cranston I had first met in the elevator. Her old working clothes comprised a turquoise blouse and stonewashed jeans, and although they were a mix of cast-offs that didn't match, she was stunningly beautiful. Not recognising the dark-haired hooker of the previous day, Jan and Arnie were incredulous, too shocked to speak. When I introduced them to Carolyn again, they both bowed a little as if she were royalty.

I showed her how to mix a gallon of each of the two paint components in the mixing pail and beat it up with the drill. 'It sets chemically, so you can't get too far ahead. When we need more paint, you mix it and tip it in our trays. Okay?'

'Sure thing. This is more interesting than boring speeches, throbbing helicopters, and security personnel so nervous they nearly shot the neighbour's cat this morning. Mind you, and there are excellent reasons for us all taking care right now, don't you think?'

'Yes, there certainly is,' said Jan.

Jan and Arnie relaxed.

Wes stayed in his car most of the time, occasionally getting out and walking the perimeter, not too evident in casual clothes. At the closest point to *Kotuku,* he watched us working, his focussed eyes the only clue to his thoughts on an otherwise deadpan face.

We completed painting one side of Arnie's hull and stopped for a break. Jan suggested to Wes that he join us for tuna sandwiches and coffee. He sat quietly, saying little, watching me closely, trying to gauge my character.

We had a radio tuned to the news, and the death toll was now over a hundred, with even more people still missing.

After Wes finished his lunch, he said, 'Thanks, Jan. That was nice. I better get back on duty. Could I have a quick word, Carolyn?'

Wes guided Carolyn a few paces away from Arnie and Jan, but a pace or so closer to me. He caught my eye as he had in the elevator.

'An unmarked car belonging to Hillier Construction has been passing by every half-hour or so,' he said. 'None of my business, of course, but I thought you should know.'

'Thanks, Wes —Not a problem—Leftie knows I'm here.'

'Another thing—but you didn't hear it from me.'

'What's that, Wes?'

'Don't look for them, but security is out there too.'

'I thought you were security?'

'I'm Secret Service, but this is something else, and I'm not in the loop. Two different cars pass by, once every hour, and their numbers don't come up in any of my usual files. There also seems to be aerial surveillance from very high up, probably authorised from even higher up, way out of my league. You'll have to use your imagination on that one. And there are other unusual vehicle movements.'

'So, who are they?'

'Dunno. My primary responsibility is for you and your safety. You know that?'

'Yes, Wes. You've been marvellous!'

'Regardless of where a threat comes from, my task is to protect you and you only.'

'What are you saying, Wes?'

'You should assume your phone is hacked; you should

assume your every move is monitored, possibly by more than one party. Hell, there are at least three other parties out there that I know of, probably more. Some may be media; some may be enemies of the state; some may be friends of the state — but not friends to you. After Oakland Bridge, everything has intensified.'

Wes paused, his eyes serious. 'You know Turnbull isn't part of the Secret Service, don't you? He dates back to the first Gulf War with the senator. Turnbull freewheels way too much as far as I'm concerned. You should trust no one, and I mean no one! Strangely, painting out here in the open, you may be safer than anywhere else. But Carolyn, please be careful!'

I didn't notice any change in Carolyn. If anything, she seemed more helpful, more enthusiastic. We finished painting Arnie's boat around 3:30 and cleaned up. We had another coffee on *Kotuku,* and the total missing or dead in California was now steady at around 220.

At about 4 pm, the straddle lifter arrived, and the driver manoeuvred his machine over the top of my boat. Five minutes later, the strops were in place, and the hydraulics whirred quietly, lifting *Kotuku* clear of the steel trestle that had supported her. But the lovely blue and white heron was not yet ready to sail. The straddle lifter trundled over to the jetty, and the driver steered it out onto the parallel piers and lowered her into the water below. She floated, still and free. I tied her to the four bollards. The crane was waiting to lift the mast upright, and that took only ten minutes. I set about tightening the mast stays while Carolyn went below and tidied cups and plates from earlier.

When I joined her, she said, 'So this is Joe's world? It is so womb-like. Do you enjoy this life, or are you hiding from something—or someone?'

'Yes, I love living on board, and if I was escaping from someone, I'm not anymore.'

Carolyn smiled. 'It's small inside; you can't exactly walk around the garden.'

'Freediving in small bays around islands in the Caribbean and Pacific makes up for that.'

'Don't you get lonely?'

'Of course, but if someone else is on board, it's up close and personal 24-7, so compatibility is important.'

'Mmm!' Carolyn seemed sombre. I waited and watched her as she slowly leafed through my music discs and old movies, smiling as she pulled the odd one out to inspect it more closely. When she turned to face me, she was serious.

'Can I tell you something, Joe?'

'Sure!'

'I can't prove it, but I believe Turnbull is behind the bombing of the Oakland Bridge. He was an explosives expert in the first Gulf War under the senator's command, and there are others from the war helping in the campaign. They call themselves the Gulf Unit. For the last few weeks, there have been secret meetings, whisperings— and other things.'

'What other things?'

'In the last two weeks, the senator has hardened up the anti-Muslim section in his campaign speeches, directly linking Obama with Osama bin Laden, and …'

'… and what?'

'Joe, when the senator's first wife died in the car bomb attack, Turnbull and the senator knew about it in advance.'

'Hell! Can you prove that?'

'Not exactly. The senator was delayed in Alaska at a meeting with Republicans, creating the perfect alibi. But I can prove Turnbull was in Santa Barbara at the time. I still have the senator's old laptop with emails on it. At the time, he told me to dump it, but I held on to it. Some emails refer to other messages that must have been deleted.'

'Where's the computer now?'

'In my wardrobe at Father's house, under my old dolls and toys.'

'Experts can retrieve deleted stuff from computers.'

'I know, but who could I trust?'

'What about Wes?'

'Wes is certainly on my side, but I'm not sure about his superiors. After lunch, he told me that my phone is probably monitored and that I am being followed everywhere by people he cannot trace.'

'Yeah, I heard most of that.'

'Now I'm apprehensive. Turnbull has said that they can do what they like once they get into power because he will control the security apparatus. It didn't worry me because the senator was never going to win. It was just hype—until the Oakland Bridge.

'And there's something else.'

I waited.

'If my phone is tapped, they know I still have the computer, because yesterday my father asked me if they knew about it. That's when I said no, emphatically not.'

I rubbed my chin. 'We could wait till dark and just sail away.'

'I'd love to—but my father is now in danger.'

Tears came to her eyes. I wrapped my arms around her, enveloping her. I liked her light perfume and brushed my lips against her hair and then lightly on her cheek.

'We have to work things out,' I said.

'This is not your problem, Joe. You should sail away—on your own!'

'Where will you be the safest tonight?'

'I don't know. I'm not going back to Cranston. But here, I put you in danger. At home, I put my father in danger ….'

'It's twilight already,' I said. 'When it's dark, we could quietly float off, go around the headland and stand offshore overnight. But that could cause other problems for you with Cranston.'

Carolyn looked into my eyes. 'Win or lose, Cranston is over for me. I have had more joy with you in a day and a half than I have had with him in three years. He may look charming, but he's a cold, hard bastard!'

I smiled. 'While we think about it, we could test the new oven I've installed. I have some nice steak in the fridge and a bottle of burgundy. Later you could ring your father to warn him.'

I went with Carolyn to tell Wes she wasn't returning with him, that he should go home to his wife for the night. Wes argued vigorously, but Carolyn was insistent. Reluctantly, Wes acceded and drove off.

Carolyn had turned my life upside down, like a rogue wave in the middle of the night or a freakish set of little waves that all simultaneously move away from your boat and crash you down into a hole. I cared about Carolyn more than I had admitted to myself, and I worried about ending our time together before it had even begun. The whole thing was turning into a *Diehard* movie, and I knew I was no Bruce Willis.

The night had darkened; a cool northerly breeze had blown up, gently rocking *Kotuku*. The marina was quiet except for the tavern adjacent to the car park, where music and laughter spread out in pleasurable ripples. Carolyn and I had eaten our meal and refilled our glasses when a short, sharp bang startled us, followed by a long whooshing noise. I was on my feet before the flash of light lit up the marina. The shock wave blew me off the hatchway steps back into the saloon. I leapt up again and could see Arnie's boat engulfed in a fireball. For just an instant, there were two moving silhouettes in the flames. I froze there, and Carolyn joined me on the steps, watching in horror as the fury of the fire consumed the small craft.

'That was meant for us, wasn't it?' she said. 'They just tried to murder us—and killed your friends, didn't they?'

'It was the new paint!' I said. 'Arnie's boat looked like *Kotuku*. On the front rank, just like we were. It was some sort of incendiary rocket, I think. We must get out of here.'

Car tyres screamed as a big limo made its exit from the marina. We leapt up onto the boat's deck. I clipped a sail end to a winch rope and commenced winding the winch, the ratchet clattering as the sail rose. 'Undo the mooring ropes!'

Carolyn released the ropes as I set the sail. The yacht, sheltering between maintenance sheds, was slow to react, easing forward nervously. The tavern had emptied, the patrons shading their eyes against the glare of the blaze.

Carolyn opened her phone. 'I have to call my father, to warn him!'

'Don't use that phone. Turn it off, right off. Power it down, so it seems dead, burnt up, and use mine or they will know you survived.'

Carolyn called her father using my cell phone, explained what had happened, and warned him that he might be in danger because of the computer. 'He wants to talk to you, Joe,' she called.

'Tell him I can't talk. Tell him we're going to run with the wind to the southeast and make as much mileage offshore as we can while it's dark. Tell him we'll call him early tomorrow and give him our position.'

I spun the wheel, tacking across the harbour towards a

container ship that had just been nudged away from the jetty by two tugs and was moving out into the shipping lane. I crossed the vessel's bow, ignoring its blasts of warning at my reckless breach of navigation rules. I turned into a course parallel to the container ship's, deliberately bringing *Kotuku* to rest, its mainsail flapping, powerless in the wind. The container ship did not alter its course or speed, and as the bow of the enormous ship drew level with the yacht, I wound hard on the winch, bringing the wind back into her sails, lifting her speed to match that of the container ship beside us. I braced for the bow wave that was about to engulf us.

'Hang on, Carolyn. It's gonna get rough for a minute, and then I'll need you up here.'

When she appeared, I said, 'Take the helm and keep her pointed at that red beacon.'

Carolyn nervously stepped up, grabbing the metre-wide wheel, bracing her feet wide. I went forward again, opening a hatch and dragging out another sail ending. I clipped it to another winch rope and returned to where Carolyn was struggling with the helm.

'It's not a car, sweetheart. You turn the helm a little and wait for her to come around, and it takes a while for her to react.' Carolyn was more like Kim Novak than Angelina Jolie, but this was more like *Tomb Raider* than *Picnic*.

I winched again, this time hoisting up the spinnaker. It filled with air in an explosive burst, the stay wires twanging, the yacht leaping forward, keeping abreast of the accelerating container ship that screened *Kotuku* from anyone watching from the marina. Police, fire engines and ambulances had appeared, creating a mass of flashing lights and screaming sirens. I trimmed the spinnaker, the boat steadied, and I took over the helm from Carolyn.

'Likely, my phone and your father's are also being

monitored, so I gave your father the wrong message about our course. I don't intend to go southeast but will tack against the wind, sailing northeast up the coastline to find somewhere to shelter—not just from the weather.'

Carolyn, still in a state of shock, nodded.

The container ship altered its course to head south, and I stayed under the spinnaker until the other vessel had disappeared into the darkness. I changed the sails again, laboriously stowing the spinnaker, and when I changed course to the northeast, *Kotuku* leaned over as it sliced into the wind, cutting through each swell, rising from each trough.

Carolyn was wet from the sea spray and shivering in the cold wind. 'You need to change. There are dry clothes below: shirts, jerseys, jackets, warm socks. They won't fit, but you should change anyway.'

'Arnie and Jan are gone, aren't they?' she said.

'Yes! I saw them—that rocket was intended for us, mainly you.'

'And you think we are still in danger?'

'Yes, but we have bought time, and time will help. Your father will see to that—I hope.'

'I hope so too.' Carolyn went below.

We moored in the lee of Pooles Island, northeast of Baltimore. The slop of the sea against the hull and the wind's singing in the rigging prevented us from listening for any water or airborne approach. We did not turn on the radio or our phones. The cloud cover gave us confidence that no one could trace us. Carolyn relaxed a little and set a Nora Jones disc on the player, and we shared the squab-covered seat in the saloon, her head on my shoulder. When the disc ended, we crawled into bed together in the main cabin. That was a lovely beginning—I thought for a while about *To Have and Have Not,* knowing how much nicer it was *to have*. Carolyn slept fitfully, tossing and turning. I held her close, and when I stroked her hair, she drifted off again.

The storm passed, and *Kotuku* lay still with a light slap-slap of the slate-grey chop on the hull. I crept from the bunk and peered skyward from the hatchway step. As the dawn sky lightened, at first just a pink wedge in the east, the sea's slop became overlaid by a distant hum. The hum steadily grew, becoming a complex pulsating throb, and three helicopters appeared over the high point of Pooles Island, slowing to face me like alien spacecraft. Apache gunships were the outer machines, with rockets slung beneath their outer fuselage and a centre-front cannon pointing straight at me. The pilots and the operators behind them were lit up by glowing instruments and screens, looking like green aliens. The helicopter in the centre was a Sea Hawk, anonymous and unarmed.

As I switched the radio on, I said to Carolyn, who had appeared at my side: 'I hope these are the good guys, or we will both be dead very soon!'

We immediately heard the call: '*Kotuku*, come in *Kotuku*.'

'*Kotuku* hears you. Please identify yourself.'

There was a brief pause and a change of voice. 'Wes here, Joe. You are in a bubble of security. Aircraft have been in the air since 2300 last night to ensure your safety. There are fighter planes riding shotgun, and overhead, an AWAC is overseeing the operation. We have enough firepower up here to start a small war.'

'We thought we were keeping a low profile,' I replied. 'We turned the radio and phones off so no one could triangulate our position.'

'Infrared imaging doesn't need radio signals, Joe. An AWAC can pick up the heat of a person from above commercial air lanes. From 30,000 feet, it could probably pick up a mouse nibbling on a piece of cheese.'

'Really!' whispered Carolyn, flushing.

'I never left the marina last night,' continued Wes, 'but stayed to keep watch. We had anticipated trouble after Carolyn's conversation with Leftie about the computer the previous day.'

Carolyn and I looked at each other in disbelief.

'We had massive backup around the marina, but we misjudged their timing and their target. We weren't expecting trouble until after the tavern closed, and we had a good cover on *Kotuku*. They were probably monitoring your phone and accelerated their plans, just screaming into the car park and firing off the rocket, not knowing you had shifted. Unfortunately, Jan and Arnie paid with their lives, but we have detained those responsible. We had your father under protection, even before you warned him last night. We secured the computer after the rocket attack, and FBI experts are already reporting sensational material.'

'Great!' I said.

'Hang on, Joe. I'll put Leftie on.'

'Leftie here. Great job, Joe. Appreciate what you've done.'

'My pleasure,' I replied, looking at Carolyn and smiling.

Wes cut back in. 'The Secret Service and Homeland Security are working under the directions of President Obama. Turnbull and others are in custody. Cranston is claiming it's a conspiracy by terrorists to destabilise the country. No one is buying his story. When we told him we were holding him for his own protection, he flipped his lid. The press is going apeshit! Voting starts in a little over twenty-four hours, and President Obama wants the rumours cleared up. He wants to lift Carolyn off your yacht for a debriefing.'

'I'll put Carolyn on,' I said.

Carolyn took the handset. 'Thanks, Wes. And thanks for looking after Father. I know I can help clarify what has happened, and I want to.'

She looked at me. 'But I won't be leaving *Kotuku* to do it. The president will have to arrange a link some other way—Skype, cell phone, whatever. Tell him to use his AWAC. And Father, I'm going to need my passport, more clothes, and some girlie stuff. Joe has asked me to go sailing with him. Our first call is *Key Largo* and maybe a small bar Joe knows in Martinique. Then we intend heading down the coast of South America.'

KISS OF THE OCEAN

EVEN IN THE protective lee of the small rocky island, we could barely hear the rattle of the descending anchor chain above the screaming wind because the evil eye of the storm had followed our path. It was hunting us down. The anchor grabbed, and we slewed around to face the storm, the old wooden charter vessel creaking and groaning as it bucked in violent spasms. As the low-pressure eye passed over us, the sea retreated on all sides—as it sometimes does—and in that instant of near calm, we dropped into the hole. The skipper cursed; a woman screamed; the rest of us gasped.

Instinctively, I plunged my hand into the end pocket of my dive bag, closing my hand on my pool goggles. The sea crashed inwards from above, crushing the cabin. The boat tried to float up. The anchor tore itself free of the prow, and water spewed in forward and aft, blowing the starboard wall outwards. I reached above my head with both arms and elbowed myself through the gap opening up between the roof and wall. The old ruptured ply splintered around me, allowing one elbow and one knee to get through. I heaved upward against the flooding water and found myself in the maelstrom, my chest and abdomen scraped and scored by the shattered ply. My clothes—no more than swim shorts and a T-shirt—had been torn from my body, leaving me as naked as the day I was born. But I was now free to kick and claw my way towards the surface, still clutching my goggles. The boat plunged downwards below me amid an upward spiralling stream of steaming water, foam and diesel fuel. The others had gone down with the wreck—instantly—all 15 of them. After a futile struggle, I assumed that I would join them but be forced to die more slowly.

My experience in the sea had started early. As a toddler, I had instantly headed for the crashing surf, each wave flattening and spilling inwards towards me like the warm frothy cream on a chocolate drink. The very first wave bowled me over. My father, close behind, scooped me up, surprised that I was laughing. I begged him to let me go free. He allowed me to float shoreward on the flat foamy water of the now-spent wave. My mother was in total panic.

'You shouldn't encourage him; it'll be his death.' I was strangely conscious of texture change, from cool damp grass to warm gritty sand, from frothy foam to the brisk sea. My love of water was instinctive, obsessive; perhaps it had originated in the warm ambient fluids of my mother's womb.

I escaped the suck of the foundering boat as it slid downwards. The explosive discharge of trapped air blew some debris outwards, and I floated freely in the heaving sea, each swell forming a crest before crashing downwards over me. Remnant rubbish and patches of viscous engine oil and diesel fuel surrounded me. I floundered, coughing out the filthy fluid, pushing away plastic floats, polystyrene bins and floating dive suits. I tried to stabilise my position. I slipped the goggles over my head in the upward lift of a rising swell, carefully spreading the straps. After the next surge, I flipped my head back and discharged the water, and settled the goggles into position. I spread my arms and feet wide, frog-like, floating but with every breaking swell crashing over me, driving me with the flow of the ocean.

As the sky darkened, the eye of the storm passed over, but the sea was still in turmoil. So far from the shore, I was at the mercy of an angry ocean. While I kept my balance with one arm, I brushed my hand across the burning broken skin of my ribcage, but the damage seemed superficial. As the current drove me past the outline of the rocky island outcrop, I knew I must avoid fighting the ocean but face my true enemies: exhaustion and hypothermia. My father had always said, 'In a bad situation, accept that the worst may happen, but try to improve the outcome.'

• • •

As a kid, I floated down the river, cold and swift from the spring snowmelt, ducking beneath overhanging willow branches and avoiding the clinging grasp of floating debris. We would sweep down the rapids among the rumbling stones as they formed ever-changing corrugations beneath us. This period filled the season between the end of winter rugby and the late October opening of the local pool that signalled summer in New Zealand.

With a coach at school and another at the club, my pool swimming rapidly improved but was tedious compared with the excitement in the sea or river. When Wes took me into his squad to hone my skills, he said, 'The slower you stroke, the faster you swim. Fast stroking is like a car skidding its tyres. All it does is burn up rubber and energy. And you must learn to swim in two dimensions.' I didn't understand what he meant, but he taught me to dip each shoulder to narrow my profile and allow my arms to go deeper to gain greater leverage. These moves forced my body to roll in the vertical plane, adding to my forward motion, snake-like. He applied this to my backstroke as well as my freestyle. 'Now you're swimming like a sleek yacht instead of a blunt barge. Have you ever watched Phelps closely? When you're ready, I'll show you how to swim in three dimensions—like Phelps.' I enjoyed my increased speed, but I still longed to see fish outlined in translucent waves that changed from jade to turquoise and watch iridescent dolphins body surfing effortlessly.

When the rain came, I rinsed my eyes, fearing the salt would close them, and I cupped my hands to drink long and slow, worrying my throat would dry out and swell up, hindering my breathing.

I could see neither the moon nor stars nor the island or the coast. I knew nothing of navigation or astronomy, but I had a sense of motion in the wild sea, a strong current driving me further north, away from New Zealand. It was pointless to gamble against nature when nature was dealing the cards. I reduced my body surface by hunching over with my knees up and my arms across my chest. I faced away from the wind and sea. I lowered energy use by keeping my lungs inflated and taking quick outward breaths, avoiding using my arms or legs to tread water. My head stayed above water except when waves broke across my back.

Time passed very slowly, but I remained calm for many hours. The rain eased, the wild wind became a light breeze, and thin slivers of light eventually signalled the coming dawn. I was cold and hungry.

During that long night, I traversed many memories. In the pool, I swam more kilometres than the length of New Zealand, perfecting splash-free stroking and feeling the soft water against my gentle palms. Wes kept his promise, teaching me the rhythms of butterfly —the three-dimensional stroke, which became my favoured mode. From a starting block, I could dolphin-kick the 50-metre length of the pool underwater. My times were improving every week and approaching national record levels, and I was four years younger than any other likely competitor.

But my pool racing came to a sudden halt. In the regional qualifications to compete at the National Championships, a rival of my coach, acting as referee, disqualified me for non-symmetrical stroking when she was at the opposite end of the pool. My coach appealed her decision, and a special hearing was convened. The president said any appeal is decided by the meet referee, the same woman who had disqualified me. She refused to reverse her ruling. The president pointed out that I had other events in which I could qualify. Instead, I told him I was withdrawing from pool swimming and would swim in the ocean with my dolphin friends, and where the only judges would be the seagulls. As I left, I could hear a bitter argument beginning between my coach and the committee.

No one supported my decision: my father was disappointed; unfortunately, my mother, who had opposed my swimming, had never seen me race, not once. Wes was angry after all of our work together. The school principal called me into his office and lectured me about loyalty; I told him I swam for myself, not the school. Even my girlfriend told me I was stupid and ended our lovely relationship. At Christmas, I gave her a necklace I had handmade by alternating white shells and blue-green paua, and I had never seen her wear it. She started dating the rugby team captain, something of a step up in her cheerleading career. She said I was oversensitive to women in authority. My friends branded me as a rebellious fool.

As the sun gradually appeared on the horizon, I flexed my limbs and body, stretching and loosening my joints. Most ocean swimmers wear a slicker suit, giving them buoyancy, insulation and reducing water resistance. None of those issues usually concerned me; I had swum in cold rivers, at wind-swept beaches, and even in the old borough pool, unfiltered, unheated, and freshly filled from the melting snow from the nearby mountain range. I rotated slowly to try and locate the coast, but my only indicators were the rising sun in the east and the earlier current flow that I had guessed was towards the north and perhaps a little to the east. I thought about the others sucked to their sudden death and wondered whether there would be a search for survivors. As the skipper had turned back to seek the island's shelter, I did not notice him use his radio, but I was not sure. He certainly had no opportunity to do so as the boat foundered.

• • •

After becoming an open water swimmer, I swam alone from the shore or went on charter trips. I avoided the competitive aspects of ocean swimming and focussed on becoming a friend of the sea: to feel the water with each palm entry allowing my rolling body to cut through the deep blue. I developed alternate composite strokes, using my arms as in breaststroke and kicking with fins as in freestyle, or dolphin kicking with the assistance of my long fins and not using my arms. Because of my breath-hold capacity, generally, I mostly used pool goggles rather than a snorkel. Without a wetsuit, I did not need a weight belt making me as sleek as a seal. Fish did not scatter before me, and dolphins often approached me, sometimes swimming with me. If I paused to inspect the underside of a boulder, some would be there beside me watching as I observed the curious behaviour of an octopus or the opening and closing of the sea anemone. I never used a speargun but collected red lobster and paua, swapping some for fish fillets speared by other more macho divers. My approach was to keep improving my skills and enjoying marine life and the cold water.

Today was very different: my time in the cold water had been cumulative; my bowel was almost empty of any nutrient. I knew that by now, my energy and warmth were being generated by the meagre supply of fatty tissue in my flesh, and those reserves were steadily diminishing. The mid-morning sea was flat, gradually turning to the south, back towards the mainland. There was a remote stretch of cloud on the horizon that I assumed to be the coastline. I did not swim but gently floated with the favourable current. A pod of dolphins casually passed me. A single little blue penguin bobbed across my path, but when he saw me, he jumped in several quick bounds out of my range, the urgency of his imagined danger lifting him clear of the water, his needs enhancing his swimming talent. Strangely, I was neither anxious about my life nor worried about my wellbeing.

My friends called me a water rat, and once a woman called me Tarzan, but I was no Johnny Weissmuller, who held every world freestyle record in real life, and who had fought a giant fake octopus in the movies. My girlfriend called me a loser; she bragged about her new boyfriend and refused to return the shell necklace. She was wearing new diamante earrings. My mother became more and more engrossed in her closed world of croquet and contract bridge as if I no longer existed.

My physics teacher had answered my question about how fish propel themselves, thoughtfully and thoroughly. 'It is about vectors; with each sway of their body, only part of the energy creates forward motion, the rest is wasted; it is quite inefficient!' He drew diagrams on the blackboard with arrows and graph lines—but I was not convinced. 'Don't they feel their way through the water, finding the favourable pressures and avoiding the unfavourable?' He shook his head in disbelief and moved on with his regular lesson. I asked the woman who taught biology the same question, and she said, 'You must live in some sort of dreamworld!'

The sea picked up some more, and the dolphins returned. They encircled me, and with the smallest of body movements, they picked up the power of the sea's surge. I joined them, slowly rather than vigorously, not energy-sapping but as enablement. It seemed as if the dolphin pod so intimately close somehow guided and assisted me; I found harmony with the moving ocean, swimming sleekly, breathing slowly, which allowed me to swim with them. Each time I emerged from my reflection to breathe, it was like the merging of sea and sky, like my first dip in the ocean. The warning words of my mother revisited me.

The presence of the dolphins was no accident. They knew the sea was rising to a swell, and we—the dolphins and I—were on the cusp of a newly forming wave. I suspected that the ocean floor, invisible below, was rising to prominence near the surface, and the dolphins were getting a free ride. So was I, body surfing as I sensed out the uplifts and forward drives among the tumult that surrounded me. I used the energy of the sea to create movement, just as beside and below me, the dolphins' bodies were virtually stationary despite their rapid forward motion.

Some dolphins went deep, then emerged, rising two or three metres above the water to draw in air. My envy drove me to try the same movement, but I only looped slightly above the surface meniscus. As the height and speed of the swell increased, I went deeper, remembering the little blue penguin increased his speed when the need arose. As I sought the surface, I dolphin kicked, and I pulled both outstretched palms back beside my flanks. Suddenly, I was in the air, above and forward of the breaking wave, with dolphins all around. I was free of all the constrictions I had always experienced—but for just a few seconds, although it seemed longer. I dipped my head between my now-outstretched arms and linked the fingers of both hands in a double fist to face the coming impact in the wave's trough five metres below. As I hit the water, I straightened my back, causing my body to rocket forward and downward. Far deeper than before, I could vaguely see the rising seabed, jagged and ugly. I used the power of the water to steer myself between protruding pinnacles on the crest of the rise. In my ecstasy, I knew I had crossed a chasm into the underwater world of my friends. Perhaps Wes would have called it the fourth dimension!

I did not struggle for air but rolled onto my back; my eyes were now red and almost closed. I had forgotten the need to breathe, but as the wave crashed past me, my speed slowed, and I found myself floating upwards into the misty foam of the broken wave. I could hear seagulls crying, perhaps watching over me, or maybe just plundering the little fish driven to the surface by the turbulence. I slowly drew air in through my swollen throat.

I had difficulty seeing the opaque sky. I wondered if I could feel cold gusts beating in the air, but I could not see anything. I lay back and thought I heard a female voice and wondered if it was real.

ABOUT THE AUTHOR

Ross Doughty has a long association with diving and fishing, with thousands of scuba and free diving experiences in New Zealand and internationally. He won his first swimming race at five years of age and now at 80, is still a Masters Champion of New Zealand. He has travelled to more than 40 countries and written five books and more than 100 blokes' stories for *Bay Fisher* magazine. He is a Life Member of the Tawa Swimming Club and Mount Maunganui Underwater Club.

Ross has a degree in English Literature from Massey University and a Master of Creative Writing from Auckland University, which received first-class honours. He lives near the sea in Auckland, New Zealand.

Contact Ross: roaldo.nz@gmail.com

OTHER BOOKS BY THE AUTHOR

The Holyoake Years

End of the Circle

Stone Octopus

Turning in the Wind

www.ingramcontent.com/pod-product-compliance
Ingram Content Group UK Ltd.
Pitfield, Milton Keynes, MK11 3LW, UK
UKHW020132250726
13967UKWH00002B/607